Way Station

Fiction reprints published by Robert Bentley, Inc.
in clothbound library editions

Way Station

CLIFFORD D. SIMAK

Robert Bentley
Cambridge, Massachusetts

Library of Congress Cataloging in Publication Data

Simak, Clifford D., 1904–
Way station.
Reprint of the ed. published by Doubleday,
Garden City, N. Y., in series:
Doubleday science fiction.
I. Title.
[PZ3.S5884Way   1979]   [PS3537.I54]   813'.5'4   79-20182
ISBN 0-8376-0440-0

Way Station

The noise was ended now. The smoke drifted like thin, gray wisps of fog above the tortured earth and the shattered fences and the peach trees that had been whittled into toothpicks by the cannon fire. For a moment silence, if not peace, fell upon those few square miles of ground where just a while before men had screamed and torn at one another in the frenzy of old hate and had contended in an ancient striving and then had fallen apart, exhausted.

For endless time, it seemed, there had been belching thunder rolling from horizon to horizon and the gouted earth that had spouted in the sky and the screams of horses and the hoarse bellowing of men; the whistling of metal and the thud when the whistle ended; the flash of searing fire and the brightness of the steel; the bravery of the colors snapping in the battle wind.

Then it all had ended and there was a silence.

But silence was an alien note that held no right upon this field or day, and it was broken by the whimper and the pain, the cry for water, and the prayer for death—the crying and the calling and the whimpering that would go on for hours beneath the summer sun. Later the huddled shapes would grow quiet and still and there would be an odor that would sicken all who passed, and the graves would be shallow graves.

There was wheat that never would be harvested, trees that would not bloom when spring came round again, and on the slope of land that ran up to the ridge the words unspoken and the deeds undone and the sodden bundles that cried aloud the emptiness and the waste of death.

There were proud names that were the prouder now, but now no more than names to echo down the ages—the Iron Brigade, the 5th New Hampshire, the 1st Minnesota, the 2nd Massachusetts, the 16th Maine.

And there was Enoch Wallace.

He still held the shattered musket and there were blisters on his hands. His face was smudged with powder. His shoes were caked with dust and blood.

He was still alive.

Dr. Erwin Hardwicke rolled the pencil back and forth between his palms, an irritating business. He eyed the man across the desk from him with some calculation.

"What I can't figure out," said Hardwicke, "is why you should come to us."

"Well, you're the National Academy and I thought . . ."

"And you're Intelligence."

"Look, Doctor, if it suits you better, let's call this visit unofficial. Pretend I'm a puzzled citizen who dropped in to see if you could help."

"It's not that I wouldn't like to help, but I don't see how I can. The whole thing is so hazy and so hypothetical."

"Damn it, man," Claude Lewis said, "you can't deny the proof —the little that I have."

"All right, then," said Hardwicke, "let's start over once again and take it piece by piece. You say you have this man . . ."

"His name," said Lewis, "is Enoch Wallace. Chronologically, he is one hundred and twenty-four years old. He was born on a farm a few miles from the town of Millville in Wisconsin, April 22, 1840, and he is the only child of Jedediah and Amanda Wallace. He enlisted among the first of them when Abe Lincoln called for volunteers. He was with the Iron Brigade, which was virtually wiped out at Gettysburg in 1863. But Wallace somehow managed to get transferred to another fighting outfit and fought down across Virginia under Grant. He was in on the end of it at Appomattox . . ."

"You've run a check on him."

"I've looked up his records. The record of enlistment at the State Capitol in Madison. The rest of it, including discharge, here in Washington."

"You say he looks like thirty."

"Not a day beyond it. Maybe even less than that."

"But you haven't talked with him."

Lewis shook his head.

"He may not be the man. If you had fingerprints . . ."

"At the time of the Civil War," said Lewis, "they'd not thought of fingerprints."

"The last of the veterans of the Civil War," said Hardwicke, "died several years ago. A Confederate drummer boy, I think. There must be some mistake."

Lewis shook his head. "I thought so myself, when I was assigned to it."

"How come you were assigned? How does Intelligence get involved in a deal like this?"

"I'll admit," said Lewis, "that it's a bit unusual. But there were so many implications . . ."

"Immortality, you mean."

"It crossed our mind, perhaps. The chance of it. But only incidentally. There were other considerations. It was a strange setup that bore some looking into."

"But Intelligence . . ."

Lewis grinned. "You are thinking, why not a scientific outfit? Logically, I suppose it should have been. But one of our men ran afoul of it. He was on vacation. Had relatives back in Wisconsin. Not in that particular area, but some thirty miles away. He heard a rumor—just the vaguest rumor, almost a casual mention. So he nosed around a bit. He didn't find out too much, but enough to make him think there might be something to it."

"That's the thing that puzzles me," said Hardwicke. "How could a man live for one hundred and twenty-four years in one locality without becoming a celebrity that the world would hear about? Can you imagine what the newspapers could do with a thing like this?"

"I shudder," Lewis said, "when I think about it."

"You haven't told me how."

"This," said Lewis, "is a bit hard to explain. You'd have to know the country and the people in it. The southwestern corner of Wisconsin is bounded by two rivers, the Mississippi on the west, the Wisconsin on the north. Away from the rivers there is flat, broad prairie land, rich land, with prosperous farms and towns. But the land that runs down to the river is rough and rugged; high hills and bluffs and deep ravines and cliffs, and there are certain areas forming bays or pockets that are isolated. They are served by inadequate roads and the small, rough farms are inhabited by a people who are closer, perhaps, to the pioneer days of a hundred years ago than they are to the twentieth century. They have cars, of course, and radios, and someday soon, perhaps, even television. But in spirit they are conservative and clannish—not all the people, of course, not even many of them, but these little isolated neighborhoods.

"At one time there were a lot of farms in these isolated pockets, but today a man can hardly make a living on a farm of that sort. Slowly the people are being squeezed out of the areas by economic circumstances. They sell their farms for whatever they can get for them and move somewhere else, to the cities mostly, where they can make a living."

Hardwicke nodded. "And the ones that are left, of course, are the most conservative and clannish."

"Right. Most of the land now is held by absentee owners who make no pretense of farming it. They may run a few head of cattle on it, but that is all. It's not too bad as a tax write-off for someone who needs that sort of thing. And in the land-bank days a lot of the land was put into the bank."

"You're trying to tell me these backwoods people—is that what you'd call them?—engaged in a conspiracy of silence."

"Perhaps not anything," said Lewis, "as formal or elaborate as that. It is just their way of doing things, a holdover from the old, stout pioneer philosophy. They minded their own business. They didn't want folks interfering with them and they interfered with no one else. If a man wanted to live to be a thousand, it might be a thing of wonder, but it was his own damned business. And if he wanted to live alone and be let alone while he was doing it, that was his business, too. They might talk about it among themselves, but to no one else. They'd resent it if some outsider tried to talk about it.

"After a time, I suppose, they came to accept the fact that Wallace kept on being young while they were growing old. The wonder wore off it and they probably didn't talk about it a great deal, even among themselves. New generations accepted it because their elders saw in it nothing too unusual—and anyhow no one saw much of Wallace because he kept strictly to himself.

"And in the nearby areas the thing, when it was thought of at all, grew to be just a sort of legend—another crazy tale that wasn't worth looking into. Maybe just a joke among those folks down Dark Hollow way. A Rip Van Winkle sort of business that probably didn't have a word of truth in it. A man might look ridiculous if he went prying into it."

"But your man looked into it."

"Yes. Don't ask me why."

"Yet he wasn't assigned to follow up the job."

"He was needed somewhere else. And besides he was known back there."

"And you?"

"It took two years of work."

"But now you know the story."

"Not all of it. There are more questions now than there were to start with."

"You've seen this man."

"Many times," said Lewis. "But I've never talked with him. I don't think he's ever seen me. He takes a walk each day before he goes to get the mail. He never moves off the place, you see. The mailman brings out the little stuff he needs. A bag of flour, a pound of bacon, a dozen eggs, cigars, and sometimes liquor."

"But that must be against the postal regulations."

"Of course it is. But mailmen have been doing it for years. It doesn't hurt a thing until someone screams about it. And no one's going to. The mailmen probably are the only friends he has ever had."

"I take it this Wallace doesn't do much farming."

"None at all. He has a little vegetable garden, but that is all he does. The place has gone back pretty much to wilderness."

"But he has to live. He must get money somewhere."

"He does," said Lewis. "Every five or ten years or so he ships off a fistful of gems to an outfit in New York."

"Legal?"

"If you mean, is it hot, I don't think so. If someone wanted to make a case of it, I suppose there are illegalities. Not to start with, when he first started sending them, back in the old days. But laws change and I suspect both he and the buyer are in defiance of any number of them."

"And you don't mind?"

"I checked on this firm," said Lewis, "and they were rather nervous. For one thing, they'd been stealing Wallace blind. I told them to keep on buying. I told them that if anyone came around to check, to refer them straight to me. I told them to keep their mouths shut and not change anything."

"You don't want anyone to scare him off," said Hardwicke.

"You're damned right, I don't. I want the mailman to keep

on acting as a delivery boy and the New York firm to keep on buying gems. I want everything to stay just the way it is. And before you ask me where the stones come from, I'll tell you I don't know."

"He maybe has a mine."

"That would be quite a mine. Diamonds and rubies and emeralds, all out of the same mine."

"I would suspect, even at the prices that he gets from them, he picks up a fair income."

Lewis nodded. "Apparently he only sends a shipment in when he runs out of cash. He wouldn't need too much. He lives rather simply, to judge from the grub he buys. But he subscribes to a lot of daily papers and news magazines and to dozens of scientific journals. He buys a lot of books."

"Technical books?"

"Some of them, of course, but mostly keeping up with new developments. Physics and chemistry and biology—all that sort of stuff."

"But I don't . . ."

"Of course you don't. Neither do I. He's no scientist. Or at least he has no formal education in the sciences. Back in the days when he went to school there wasn't much of it—not in the sense of today's scientific education. And whatever he learned then would be fairly worthless now in any event. He went through grade school—one of those one-room country schools— and spent one winter at what was called an academy that operated for a year or two down in Millville village. In case you don't know, that was considerably better than par back in the 1850s. He was, apparently, a fairly bright young man."

Hardwicke shook his head. "It sounds incredible. You've checked on all of this?"

"As well as I could. I had to go at it gingerly. I wanted no one to catch on. And one thing I forgot—he does a lot of writing. He buys these big, bound record books, in lots of a dozen at the time. He buys ink by the pint."

Hardwicke got up from his desk and paced up and down the room.

"Lewis," he said, "if you hadn't shown me your credentials and if I hadn't checked on them, I'd figure all of this to be a very tasteless joke."

He went back and sat down again. He picked up the pencil and started rolling it between his palms once more.

"You've been on the case two years," he said. "You have no ideas?"

"Not a one," said Lewis. "I'm entirely baffled. That is why I'm here."

"Tell me more of his history. After the war, that is."

"His mother died," said Lewis, "while he was away. His father and the neighbors buried her right there on the farm. That was the way a lot of people did it then. Young Wallace got a furlough, but not in time to get home for the funeral. There wasn't much embalming done in those days and the traveling was slow. Then he went back to the war. So far as I can find, it was his only furlough. The old man lived alone and worked the farm, batching it and getting along all right. From what I can pick up, he was a good farmer, an exceptionally good farmer for his day. He subscribed to some farm journals and was progressive in his ideas. He paid attention to such things as crop rotation and the prevention of erosion. The farm wasn't much of a farm by modern standards, but it made him a living and a little extra he managed to lay by.

"Then Enoch came home from the war and they farmed the place together for a year or so. The old man bought a mower—one of those horse-drawn contraptions with a sickle bar to cut hay or grain. It was the progressive thing to do. It beat a scythe all hollow.

"Then one afternoon the old man went out to mow a hayfield. The horses ran away. Something must have scared them. Enoch's father was thrown off the seat and forward, in front of the sickle bar. It was not a pretty way to die."

Hardwicke made a grimace of distaste. "Horrible," he said.

"Enoch went out and gathered up his father and got the body to the house. Then he took a gun and went hunting for the horses. He found them down in the corner of the pasture and he shot the two of them and he left them. I mean exactly that. For years their skeletons lay there in the pasture, where he'd killed them, still hitched to the mower until the harness rotted.

"Then he went back to the house and laid his father out. He washed him and he dressed him in the good black suit and laid him on a board, then went out to the barn and carpentered a coffin. And after that, he dug a grave beside his mother's grave. He finished it by lantern light, then went back to the house and sat up with his father. When morning came, he went to tell the nearest neighbor and that neighbor notified the others and someone went to get a preacher. Late in the afternoon they had the funeral, and Enoch went back to the house. He has lived there ever since, but he never farmed the land. Except the garden, that is."

"You told me these people wouldn't talk to strangers. You seem to have learned a lot."

"It took two years to do it. I infiltrated them. I bought a beat-up car and drifted into Millville and I let it out that I was a ginseng hunter."

"A what?"

"A ginseng hunter. Ginseng is a plant."

"Yes, I know. But there's been no market for it for years."

"A small market and an occasional one. Exporters will take on some of it. But I hunted other medicinal plants as well and pretended an extensive knowledge of them and their use. 'Pretended' isn't actually the word; I boned up plenty on them."

"The kind of simple soul," said Hardwicke, "those folks could understand. A sort of cultural throwback. And inoffensive, too. Perhaps not quite right in the head."

Lewis nodded. "It worked even better than I thought. I just wandered around and people talked to me. I even found some ginseng. There was one family in particular—the Fisher family. They live down in the river bottoms below the Wallace farm, which sits on the ridge above the bluffs. They've lived there almost as long as the Wallace family, but a different stripe entirely. The Fishers are a coon-hunting, catfishing, moonshine-cooking tribe. They found a kindred spirit in me. I was just as shiftless and no-account as they were. I helped them with their moonshine, both in the making and the drinking and once in a while the peddling. I went fishing with them and hunting with them and I sat around and talked and they showed me a place or two where I might find some ginseng—'sang' is what they call it. I imagine a social scientist might find a gold mine in the Fishers. There is one girl—a deaf-mute, but a pretty thing, and she can charm off warts . . ."

"I recognize the type," said Hardwicke. "I was born and raised in the southern mountains."

"They were the ones who told me about the team and mower. So one day I went up in that corner of the Wallace pasture and did some digging. I found a horse's skull and some other bones."

"But no way of knowing if it was one of the Wallace horses."

"Perhaps not," said Lewis. "But I found part of the mower as well. Not much left of it, but enough to identify."

"Let's get back to the history," suggested Hardwicke. "After the father's death, Enoch stayed on at the farm. He never left it?"

Lewis shook his head. "He lives in the same house. Not a thing's been changed. And the house apparently has aged no more than the man."

"You've been in the house?"

"Not in it. At it. I will tell you how it was."

3

He had an hour. He knew he had an hour, for he had timed Enoch Wallace during the last ten days. And from the time he left the house until he got back with his mail, it had never been less than an hour. Sometimes a little longer, when the mailman might be late, or they got to talking. But an hour, Lewis told himself, was all that he could count on.

Wallace had disappeared down the slope of ridge, heading for the point of rocks that towered above the bluff face, with the Wisconsin River running there below. He would climb the rocks and stand there, with the rifle tucked beneath his arm, to gaze across the wilderness of the river valley. Then he would go back down the rocks again and trudge along the wooded path to where, in proper season, the pink lady's-slippers grew, and from there up the hill again to the spring that gushed out of the hillside just below the ancient field that had lain fallow for a century or more, and then along the slope until he hit the almost overgrown road and so down to the mailbox.

In the ten days that Lewis had watched him, his route had never varied. It was likely, Lewis told himself, that it had not varied through the years. Wallace did not hurry. He walked as if he had all the time there was. And he stopped along the way to renew acquaintances with old friends of his—a tree, a squirrel, a flower. He was a rugged man and there still was much of the soldier in him—old tricks and habits left from the bitter years of campaigning under many leaders. He walked with his head held high and his shoulders back and he moved with the easy stride of one who had known hard marches.

Lewis came out of the tangled mass of trees that once had been an orchard and in which a few trees, twisted and gnarled and gray with age, still bore their pitiful and bitter crop of apples.

He stopped at the edge of the copse and stood for a moment to stare up at the house on the ridge above, and for a single instant it seemed to him the house stood in a special light, as if a rare and more distilled essence of the sun had crossed the gulf of space to shine upon this house and to set it apart from all other houses in the world. Bathed in that light, the house was somehow unearthly, as if, indeed, it might be set apart as a very special thing. And then the light, if it ever had been there, was gone and the house shared the common sunlight of the fields and woods.

Lewis shook his head and told himself that it had been foolishness, or perhaps a trick of seeing. For there was no such thing as special sunlight and the house was no more than a house, although wondrously preserved.

It was the kind of house one did not see too often in these days. It was rectangular; long and narrow and high, with old-fashioned gingerbread along the eaves and gables. It had a certain gauntness that had nothing to do with age; it had been gaunt the day it had been built—gaunt and plain and strong, like the people that it sheltered. But gaunt as it might be, it stood prim and neat, with no peeling paint, with no sign of weathering, and no hint of decay.

Against one end of it was a smaller building, no more than a shed, as if it were an alien structure that had been carted in from some other place and shoved against its end, covering the side door of the house. Perhaps the door, thought Lewis, that led into the kitchen. The shed undoubtedly had been used as a place to hang outdoor clothing and to leave overshoes and boots, with a bench for milk cans and buckets, and perhaps a basket in which to gather eggs. From the top of it extended some three feet of stovepipe.

Lewis went up to the house and around the shed and there, in the side of it, was a door ajar. He stepped up on the stoop and pushed the door wide open and stared in amazement at the room.

For it was not a simple shed. It apparently was the place where Wallace lived.

The stove from which the stovepipe projected stood in one corner, an ancient cookstove, smaller than the old-fashioned kitchen range. Sitting on its top was a coffeepot, a frying pan, and a griddle. Hung from hooks on a board behind it were other cooking implements. Opposite the stove, shoved against the wall, was a three-quarter-size four-poster bed, covered with a lumpy quilt, quilted in one of the ornate patterns of many pieces of many-colored cloth, such as had been the delight of ladies of a century before. In another corner was a table and a chair, and above the table, hung against the wall, a small open cupboard in which were stacked some dishes. On the table stood a kerosene lantern, battered from much usage, but with its chimney clean, as if it had been washed and polished as recently as this morning.

There was no door into the house, no sign there had ever been a door. The clapboard of the house's outer wall ran unbroken to form the fourth wall of the shed.

This was incredible, Lewis told himself—that there should be no door, that Wallace should live here, in this shed, when there was a house to live in. As if there were some reason he should not occupy the house, and yet must stay close by it. Or perhaps that he might be living out a penance of some sort, living here in this shed as a medieval hermit might have lived in a woodland hut or in a desert cave.

He stood in the center of the shed and looked around him, hoping that he might find some clue to this unusual circumstance. But there was nothing, beyond the bare, hard fact of living, the very basic necessities of living—the stove to cook his food and heat the place, the bed to sleep on, the table to eat on, and the lantern for its light. Not even so much as an extra hat (although, come to think of it, Wallace never wore a hat) or an extra coat.

No sign of magazines or papers, and Wallace never came home from the mailbox empty-handed. He subscribed to the New York *Times,* the *Wall Street Journal,* the *Christian Science Monitor,* and the Washington *Star,* as well as many scientific and technical journals. But there was no sign of them here, nor of the many books he bought. No sign, either, of the bound record books. Nothing at all on which a man could write.

Perhaps, Lewis told himself, this shed, for some baffling reason, was no more than a show place, a place staged most carefully to make one think that this was where Wallace lived. Perhaps, after all, he lived in the house. Although, if that were the case, why all this effort, not too successful, to make one think he didn't?

Lewis turned to the door and walked out of the shed. He went around the house until he reached the porch that led up to the front door. At the foot of the steps, he stopped and looked around. The place was quiet. The sun was midmorning-high and the day was warming up and this sheltered corner of the earth stood relaxed and hushed, waiting for the heat.

He looked at his watch and he had forty minutes left, so he went up the steps and across the porch until he came to the door. Reaching out his hand, he grasped the knob and turned— except he didn't turn it; the knob stayed exactly where it was and his clenched fingers went half around it in the motion of a turn.

Puzzled, he tried again and still he didn't turn the knob. It was as if the knob were covered with some hard, slick coating, like a coat of brittle ice, on which the fingers slipped without exerting any pressure on the knob.

He bent his head close to the knob and tried to see if there were any evidence of coating, and there was no evidence. The knob looked perfectly all right—too all right, perhaps. For it was clean, as if someone had wiped and polished it. There was no dust upon it, and no weather specks.

He tried a thumbnail on it, and the thumbnail slipped but left no mark behind it. He ran his palm over the outer surface of the door and the wood was slick. The rubbing of the palm set up no friction. The palm slid along the wood as if the palm were greased, but there was no sign of grease. There was no indication of anything to account for the slickness of the door.

Lewis moved from the door to the clapboard and the clapboard also was slick. He tried palm and thumbnail on it and the answer was the same. There was something covering this house which made it slick and smooth—so smooth that dust could not cling upon its surface nor could weather stain it.

He moved along the porch until he came to a window, and now, as he stood facing the window, he realized something he had not noticed before, something that helped make the house seem gaunter than it really was. The windows were black. There were no curtains, no drapes, no shades; they were simply black rectangles, like empty eyes staring out of the bare skull of the house.

He moved closer to the window and put his face up to it, shading the sides of his face, next to the eyes, with his upheld hands to shield out the sunlight. But even so, he could not see into the room beyond. He stared, instead, into a pool of blackness, and the blackness, curiously enough, had no reflective qualities. He could not see himself reflected in the glass. He could see nothing but the blackness, as if the light hit the window and was absorbed by it, sucked in and held by it. There was no bouncing back of light once it had hit that window.

He left the porch and went slowly around the house, examining it as he went. The windows were all blank, black pools that sucked in the captured light, and all the exterior was slick and hard.

He pounded the clapboard with his fist, and it was like the pounding of a rock. He examined the stone walls of the basement where they were exposed, and the walls were smooth and slick. There were mortar gaps between the stones and in the stones themselves one could see uneven surfaces, but the hand rubbed across the wall could detect no roughness.

An invisible something had been laid over the roughness of the stone, just enough of it to fill in the pits and uneven surfaces. But one could not detect it. It was almost as if it had no substance.

Straightening up from his examination of the wall, Lewis looked at his watch. There were only ten minutes left. He must be getting on.

He walked down the hill toward the tangle of old orchard. At its edge he stopped and looked back, and now the house was different. It was no longer just a structure. It wore a personality, a mocking, leering look, and there was a malevolent chuckle bubbling inside of it, ready to break out.

Lewis ducked into the orchard and worked his way in among the trees. There was no path and beneath the trees the grass and weeds grew tall. He ducked the drooping branches and walked around a tree that had been uprooted in some windstorm of many years before.

He reached up as he went along, picking an apple here and there, scrubby things and sour, taking a single bite out of each one of them, then throwing it away, for there was none of them that was fit to eat, as if they might have taken from the neglected soil a certain basic bitterness.

At the far side of the orchard he found the fence and the graves that it enclosed. Here the weeds and grass were not so high and the fence showed signs of repair made rather recently, and at the foot of each grave, opposite the three crude native limestone headstones, was a peony bush, each a great straggling mass of plants that had grown, undisciplined, for years.

Standing before the weathered picketing, he knew that he had stumbled on the Wallace family burial plot.

But there should have been only the two stones. What about the third?

He moved around the fence to the sagging gate and went into the plot. Standing at the foot of the graves, he read the legends on the stones. The carving was angular and rough, giving evidence of having been executed by unaccustomed hands. There were no pious phrases, no lines of verse, no carvings of angels or of lambs or of other symbolic figures such as had been customary in the 1860s. There were just the names and dates.

On the first stone: Amanda Wallace 1821–1863

And on the second stone: Jedediah Wallace 1816–1866

And on the third stone——

4

"Give me that pencil, please," said Lewis.

Hardwicke quit rolling it between his palms and handed it across.

"Paper, too?" he asked.

"If you please," said Lewis.

He bent above the desk and drew rapidly.

"Here," he said, handing back the paper.

Hardwicke wrinkled his brow.

"But it makes no sense," he said. "Except for that figure underneath."

"The figure eight, lying on its side. Yes, I know. The symbol for infinity."

"But the rest of it?"

"I don't know," said Lewis. "It is the inscription on the tombstone. I copied it . . ."

"And you know it now by heart."

"I should. I've studied it enough."

"I've never seen anything like it in my life," said Hardwicke. "Not that I'm an authority. I really know little at all in this field."

"You can put your mind at rest. It's nothing that anyone knows anything about. It bears no resemblance, not even the remotest, to any language or any known inscription. I checked with men who know. Not one, but a dozen of them. I told them I'd found it on a rocky cliff. I am sure that most of them think I am a crackpot. One of those people who are trying to prove that the Romans or the Phoenicians or the Irish or whatnot had pre-Colombian settlements in America."

Hardwicke put down the sheet of paper.

"I can see what you mean," he said, "when you say you have more questions now than when you started. Not only the question of a young man more than a century old, but likewise the matter of the slickness of the house and the third gravestone with the undecipherable inscription. You say you've never talked with Wallace?"

"No one talks to him. Except the mailman. He goes out on his daily walks and he packs this gun."

"People are afraid to talk with him?"

"Because of the gun, you mean."

"Well, yes, I suppose that was in the back of my mind. I wondered why he carried it."

Lewis shook his head. "I don't know. I've tried to tie it in, to find some reason he always has it with him. He has never fired the rifle so far as I can find. But I don't think the rifle is the reason no one talks with him. He's an anachronism, something living from another age. No one fears him, I am sure of that. He's been around too long for anyone to fear him. Too familiar. He's a fixture of the land, like a tree or boulder. And yet no one feels quite comfortable with him, either. I would imagine that most of them, if they should come face to face with him, would feel uncomfortable. For he's something they are not—something greater than they are and at the same time a good deal less. As

if he were a man who had walked away from his own humanity.
I think that, secretly, many of his neighbors may be a bit ashamed
of him, shamed because he has, somehow, perhaps ignobly, side-
stepped growing old, one of the penalties, but perhaps, as well,
one of the rights of all humankind. And perhaps this secret shame
may contribute in some part to their unwillingness to talk about
him."

"You spent a good deal of time watching him?"

"There was a time I did. But now I have a crew. They watch
on regular shifts. We have a dozen spots we watch from, and
we keep shifting them around. There isn't an hour, day in, day
out, that the Wallace house isn't under observation."

"This business really has you people bugged."

"I think with reason," Lewis said. "There is still one other
thing."

He bent over and picked up the brief case he had placed
beside his chair. Unsnapping it, he took out a sheaf of photo-
graphs and handed them to Hardwicke.

"What do you make of these?" he asked.

Hardwicke picked them up. Suddenly he froze. The color
drained out of his face. His hands began to tremble and he laid
the pictures carefully on the desk. He had looked at only the
top one; not any of the others.

Lewis saw the question in his face.

"In the grave," he said. "The one beneath the headstone with
the funny writing."

5

The message machine whistled shrilly, and Enoch
Wallace put away the book in which he had been writing and
got up from his desk. He walked across the room to the whistling

machine. He punched a button and shoved a key and the whistling stopped.

The machine built up its hum and the message began to form on the plate, faint at first and then becoming darker until it stood out clearly. It read:

NO. 406301 TO STATION 18327. TRAVELER AT 16097.38. NATIVE THUBAN VI. NO BAGGAGE. NO. 3 LIQUID TANK. SOLUTION 27. DEPART FOR STATION 12892 AT 16439.16. CONFIRM.

Enoch glanced up at the great galactic chronometer hanging on the wall. There was almost three hours to go.

He touched a button, and a thin sheet of metal bearing the message protruded from the side of the machine. Beneath it the duplicate fed itself into the record file. The machine chuckled and the message plate was clear once more and waiting.

Enoch pulled out the metal plate, threaded the holes in it through the double filing spindle and then dropped his fingers to the keyboard and typed: NO. 406301 RECEIVED. CONFIRM MOMENTARILY. The message came into being on the plate and he left it there.

Thuban VI? Had there been, he wondered, one of them before? As soon as he got his chores done, he would go to the filing cabinet and check.

It was a liquid tank case and those, as a rule, were the most uninteresting of all. They usually were hard ones to strike up a conversation with, because too often their concept of language was too difficult to handle. And as often, too, their very thinking processes proved too divergent to provide much common ground for communication.

Although, he recalled, that was not always true. There had been that tank traveler several years ago, from somewhere in Hydra (or had it been the Hyades?), he'd sat up the whole night with and almost failed of sending off on time, yarning through the hours, their communication (you couldn't call it words) tumbling over one another as they packed into the little time they had a lot of fellowship and, perhaps, some brotherhood.

He, or she, or it—they'd never got around to that—had not come back again. And that was the way it was, thought Enoch; very few came back. By far the greater part of them were just passing through.

But he had he, or she, or it (whichever it might be) down in black and white, as he had all of them, every single blessed one of them, down in black and white. It had taken him, he remembered, almost the entire following day, crouched above his desk, to get it written down; all the stories he'd been told, all the glimpses he had caught of a far and beautiful and tantalizing land (tantalizing because there was so much of it he could not understand), all the warmth and comradeship that had flowed between himself and this misshapen, twisted, ugly living being from another world. And any time he wished, any day he wished, he could take down the journal from the row of journals and relive that night again. Although he never had. It was strange, he thought, how there was never time, or never seemed to be the time, to thumb through and reread in part what he'd recorded through the years.

He turned from the message machine and rolled a No. 3 liquid tank into place beneath the materializer, positioning it exactly and locking it in place. Then he pulled out the retracting hose and thumbed the selector over to No. 27. He filled the tank and let the hose slide back into the wall.

Back at the machine, he cleared the plate and sent off his confirmation that all was ready for the traveler from Thuban, got back double confirmation from the other end, then threw the machine to neutral, ready to receive again.

He went from the machine to the filing cabinet that stood next to his desk and pulled out a drawer jammed with filing cards. He looked and Thuban VI was there, keyed to August 22, 1931. He walked across the room to the wall filled with books and rows of magazines and journals, filled from floor to ceiling, and found the record book he wanted. Carrying it, he walked back to his desk.

August 22, 1931, he found, when he located the entry, had been one of his lighter days. There had been one traveler only, the one from Thuban VI. And although the entry for the day filled almost a page in his small, crabbed writing, he had devoted no more than one paragraph to the visitor.

Came today [it read] *a blob from Thuban VI. There is no other way in which one might describe it. It is simply a mass of matter, presumably of flesh, and this mass seems to go through some sort of rhythmic change in shape, for periodically it is globular, then begins to flatten out until it lies in the bottom of the tank, somewhat like a pancake. Then it begins to contract and to pull in upon itself, until finally it is a ball again. This change is rather slow and definitely rhythmic, but only in the sense that it follows the same pattern. It seems to have no relation to time. I tried timing it and could detect no time pattern. The shortest period needed to complete the cycle was seven minutes and the longest was eighteen. Perhaps over a longer period one might be able to detect a time rhythm, but I didn't have the time. The semantic translator did not work with it, but it did emit for me a series of sharp clicks, as if it might be clicking claws together, although it had no claws that I could see. When I looked this up in the pasimology manual I learned that what it was trying to say was that it was all right, that it needed no attention, and please leave it alone. Which I did thereafter.*

And at the end of the paragraph, jammed into the little space that had been left, was the notation: *See Oct. 16, 1931.*

He turned the pages until he came to October 16 and that had been one of the days, he saw, that Ulysses had arrived to inspect the station.

His name, of course, was not Ulysses. As a matter of fact, he had no name at all. Among his people there was no need of names; there was other identifying terminology which was far more expressive than mere names. But this terminology, even the very concept of it, was such that it could not be grasped, much less put to use, by human beings.

"I shall call you Ulysses," Enoch recalled telling him, the first time they had met. "I need to call you something."

"It is agreeable," said the then strange being (but no longer strange). "Might one ask why the name Ulysses?"

"Because it is the name of a great man of my race."

"I am glad you chose it," said the newly christened being. "To my hearing it has a dignified and noble sound and, between the two of us, I shall be glad to bear it. And I shall call you Enoch, for the two of us shall work together for many of your years."

And it had been many years, thought Enoch, with the record book open to that October entry of more than thirty years ago. Years that had been satisfying and enriching in a way that one could not have imagined until it had all been laid out before him.

And it would go on, he thought, much longer than it already had gone on—for many centuries more, for a thousand years, perhaps. And at the end of that thousand years, what would he know then?

Although, perhaps, he thought, the knowing was not the most important part of it.

And none of it, he knew, might come to pass, for there was interference now. There were watchers, or at least a watcher, and before too long whoever it might be might start closing in. What he'd do or how he'd meet the threat, he had no idea until that moment came. It was something that had been almost bound to happen. It was something he had been prepared to have happen all these years. There was some reason to wonder, he knew, that it had not happened sooner.

He had told Ulysses of the danger of it that first day they'd met. He'd been sitting on the steps that led up to the porch, and thinking of it now, he could remember it as clearly as if it had been only yesterday.

6

He was sitting on the steps and it was late afternoon. He was watching the great white thunderheads that were piling up across the river beyond the Iowa hills. The day was hot and sultry and there was not a breath of moving air. Out in the barnyard a half a dozen bedraggled chickens scratched listlessly, for the sake, it seemed, of going through the motions rather than from any hope of finding food. The sound of the sparrows' wings, as they flew between the gable of the barn and the hedge of honeysuckle that bordered the field beyond the road, was a harsh, dry sound, as if the feathers of their wings had grown stiff with heat.

And here he sat, he thought, staring at the thunderheads when there was work to do—corn to be plowed and hay to be gotten in and wheat to reap and shock.

For despite whatever might have happened, a man still had a life to live, days to be gotten through the best that one could manage. It was a lesson, he reminded himself, that he should have learned in all its fullness in the last few years. But war, somehow, was different from what had happened here. In war you knew it and expected it and were ready when it happened, but this was not the war. This was the peace to which he had returned. A man had a right to expect that in the world of peace there really would be peace fencing out the violence and the horror.

Now he was alone, as he'd never been alone before. Now, if ever, could be a new beginning; now, perhaps, there had to be a new beginning. But whether it was here, on the homestead acres, or in some other place, it still would be a beginning of bitterness and anguish.

He sat on the steps, with his wrists resting on his knees, and watched the thunderheads piling in the west. It might mean rain and the land could use the rain—or it might be nothing, for above the merging river valleys the air currents were erratic and there was no way a man could tell where those clouds might flow.

He did not see the traveler until he turned in at the gate. He was a tall and gangling one and his clothes were dusty and from the appearance of him he had walked a far way. He came up the path and Enoch sat waiting for him, watching him, but not stirring from the steps.

"Good day, sir," Enoch finally said. "It's a hot day to be walking. Why don't you sit a while."

"Quite willingly," said the stranger. "But first, I wonder, could I have a drink of water?"

Enoch got up to his feet. "Come along," he said. "I'll pump a fresh one for you."

He went down across the barnyard until he reached the pump. He unhooked the dipper from where it hung upon a bolt and handed it to the man. He grasped the handle of the pump and worked it up and down.

"Let it run a while," he said. "It takes a time for it to get real cool."

The water splashed out of the spout, running on the boards that formed the cover of the well. It came in spurts as Enoch worked the handle.

"Do you think," the stranger asked, "that it is about to rain?"

"A man can't tell," said Enoch. "We have to wait and see."

There was something about this traveler that disturbed him. Nothing, actually, that one could put a finger on, but a certain strangeness that was vaguely disquieting. He watched him narrowly as he pumped and decided that probably this stranger's ears were just a bit too pointed at the top, but put it down to his imagination, for when he looked again they seemed to be all right.

"I think," said Enoch, "that the water should be cold by now."

The traveler put down the dipper and waited for it to fill. He offered it to Enoch. Enoch shook his head.

"You first. You need it worse than I do."

The stranger drank greedily and with much slobbering.

"Another one?" asked Enoch.

"No, thank you," said the stranger. "But I'll catch another dipperful for you if you wish me to."

Enoch pumped, and when the dipper was full the stranger handed it to him. The water was cold and Enoch, realizing for the first time that he had been thirsty, drank it almost to the bottom.

He hung the dipper back on its bolt and said to the man, "Now, let's get in that sitting."

The stranger grinned. "I could do with some of it," he said. Enoch pulled a red bandanna from his pocket and mopped his face. "The air gets close," he said, "just before a rain."

And as he mopped his face, quite suddenly he knew what it was that had disturbed him about the traveler. Despite his bedraggled clothes and his dusty shoes, which attested to long walking, despite the heat of this time-before-a-rain, the stranger was not sweating. He appeared as fresh and cool as if he had been lying at his ease beneath a tree in springtime.

Enoch put the bandanna back into his pocket and they walked back to the steps and sat there, side by side.

"You've traveled a far way," said Enoch, gently prying.

"Very far, indeed," the stranger told him. "I'm a right smart piece from home."

"And you have a far way yet to go?"

"No," the stranger said, "I believe that I have gotten to the place where I am going."

"You mean . . ." asked Enoch, and left the question hanging.

"I mean right here," said the stranger, "sitting on these steps. I have been looking for a man and I think that man is you. I did not know his name nor where to look for him, but yet I knew that one day I would find him."

"But me," Enoch said, astonished. "Why should you look for me?"

"I was looking for a man of many different parts. One of the things about him was that he must have looked up at the stars and wondered what they were."

"Yes," said Enoch, "that is something I have done. On many nights, camping in the field, I have lain in my blankets and looked up at the sky, looking at the stars and wondering what they were and how they'd been put up there and, most important of all, why they had been put up there. I have heard some say that each of them is another sun like the sun that shines on Earth, but I don't know about that. I guess there is no one who knows too much about them."

"There are some," the stranger said, "who know a deal about them."

"You, perhaps," said Enoch, mocking just a little, for the stranger did not look like a man who'd know much of anything.

"Yes, I," the stranger said. "Although I do not know as much as many others do."

"I've sometimes wondered," Enoch said, "if the stars are other suns, might there not be other planets and other people, too."

He remembered sitting around the campfire of a night, jawing with the other fellows to pass away the time. And once he'd mentioned this idea of maybe other people on other planets circling other suns and the fellows all had jeered him and for days afterward had made fun of him, so he had never mentioned it again. Not that it mattered much, for he had no real belief in it himself; it had never been more than campfire speculation.

And now he'd mentioned it again and to an utter stranger. He wondered why he had.

"You believe that?" asked the stranger.

Enoch said, "It was just an idle notion."

"Not so idle," said the stranger. "There are other planets and there are other people. I am one of them."

"But you . . ." cried Enoch, then was stricken into silence.

For the stranger's face had split and began to fall away and beneath it he caught the glimpse of another face that was not a human face.

And even as the false human face sloughed off that other face, a great sheet of lightning went crackling across the sky and the heavy crash of thunder seemed to shake the land and from far off he heard the rushing of the rain as it charged across the hills.

7

That was how it started, Enoch thought, almost a hundred years ago. The campfire fantasy had turned into fact and the Earth now was on galactic charts, a way station for many different peoples traveling star to star. Strangers once, but now there were no strangers. There were no such things as strangers. In whatever form, with whatever purpose, all of them were people.

He looked back at the entry for October 16, 1931, and ran through it swiftly. There, near the end of it was the sentence:

Ulysses says the Thubans from planet VI are perhaps the greatest mathematicians in the galaxy. They have developed, it seems, a numeration system superior to any in existence, especially valuable in the handling of statistics.

He closed the book and sat quietly in the chair, wondering if the statisticians of Mizar X knew of the Thubans' work. Perhaps they did, he thought, for certainly some of the math they used was unconventional.

He pushed the record book to one side and dug into a desk drawer, bringing out his chart. He spread it flat on the desk before him and puzzled over it. If he could be sure, he thought. If he only knew the Mizar statistics better. For the last ten years or more he had labored at the chart, checking and rechecking all the factors against the Mizar system, testing again and again to determine whether the factors he was using were the ones he should be using.

He raised a clenched fist and hammered at the desk. If he only could be certain. If he could only talk with someone. But that had been something that he had shrank from doing, for it would be equivalent to showing the very nakedness of the human race.

He still was human. Funny, he thought, that he should stay human, that in a century of association with these beings from the many stars he should have, through it all, remained a man of Earth.

For in many ways, his ties with Earth were cut. Old Winslowe Grant was the only human he ever talked with now. His neighbors shunned him, and there were no others, unless one could count the watchers, and those he seldom saw—only glimpses of them, only the places they had been.

Only old Winslowe Grant and Mary and the other people from the shadow who came occasionally to spend lonely hours with him.

That was all of Earth he had, old Winslowe and the shadow people and the homestead acres that lay outside the house—but not the house itself, for the house was alien now.

He shut his eyes and remembered how the house had been in the olden days. There had been a kitchen, in this same area where he was sitting, with the iron cookstove, black and monstrous, in its corner, showing its row of fiery teeth along the slit made by the grate. Pushed against the wall had been the table where the three of them had eaten, and he could remember how the table looked, with the vinegar cruet and the glass that held the spoons and the Lazy Susan with the mustard, horse-radish, and chili sauce sitting in a group, a sort of centerpiece in the middle of the red checkered cloth that the table wore.

There had been a winter night and he had been, it seemed, no more than three or four. His mother was busy at the stove with supper. He was sitting on the floor in the center of the kitchen, playing with some blocks, and outside he could hear the muffled howling of the wind as it prowled along the eaves. His father had come in from milking at the barn, and a gust of wind and a swirl of snow had come into the room with him. Then he'd shut the door and the wind and snow were gone, shut outside this house, condemned to the outer darkness and the wilderness of night. His father had set the pail of milk that he had been carrying on the kitchen sink and Enoch saw that his beard and eyebrows were coated with snow and there was frost on the whiskers all around his mouth.

He held that picture still, the three of them like historic mani-kins posed in a cabinet in a museum—his father with the frost upon his whiskers and the great felt boots that came up to his knees; his mother with her face flushed from working at the stove and with the lace cap upon her head, and himself upon the floor, playing with the blocks.

There was one other thing that he remembered, perhaps more clearly than all the rest of it. There was a great lamp sitting on the table, and on the wall behind it hung a calendar, and the glow of the lamp fell like a spotlight upon the picture on the calendar. There was old Santa Claus, riding in his sleigh along a woodland track and all the little woodland people had turned out to watch him pass. A great moon hung above the trees and there was thick snow on the ground. A pair of rabbits sat there, gazing soulfully at Santa, and a deer beside the rabbits, with a raccoon just a little distance off, ringed tail wrapped about his feet, and a squirrel and chickadee side by side upon an overhanging branch. Old Santa had his whip raised high in greeting and his cheeks were red and his smile was merry and the reindeer hitched to his sled were fresh and spirited and proud.

Through all the years this mid-nineteenth-century Santa had ridden down the snowy aisles of time, with his whip uplifted in happy greeting to the woodland creatures. And the golden lamplight had ridden with him, still bright upon the wall and the checkered tablecloth.

So, thought Enoch, some things do endure—the memory and the thought and the snug warmness of a childhood kitchen on a stormy winter night.

But the endurance was of the spirit and the mind, for nothing else endured. There was no kitchen now, nor any sitting room with its old-fashioned sofa and the rocking chair; no back parlor with its stuffy elegance of brocade and silk, no guest bedroom on the first and no family bedrooms on the second floor.

It all was gone and now one room remained. The second-story floor and all partitions had been stripped away. Now the house was one great room. One side of it was the galactic station and the other side the living space for the keeper of the station. There was a bed over in one corner and a stove that worked on no principle known on Earth and a refrigerator that was of alien make. The walls were lined with cabinets and shelves, stacked with magazines and books and journals.

There was just one thing left from the early days, the one thing Enoch had not allowed the alien crew that had set up the station to strip away—the massive old fireplace of brick and native stone that had stood against one wall of the sitting room. It still stood there, the one reminder of the days of old, the one thing left of Earth, with its great, scarred oak mantel that his father had carved out with a broadax from a massive log and had smoothed by hand with plane and draw-shave.

On the fireplace mantel and strewn on shelf and table were articles and artifacts that had no earthly origin and some no earthly names—the steady accumulation through the years of the gifts from friendly travelers. Some of them were functional and others were to look at only, and there were other things that were entirely useless because they had little application to a member of the human race or were inoperable on Earth, and many others of the purpose of which he had no idea, accepting them, embarrassed, with many stumbling thanks, from the well-meaning folks who had brought them to him.

And on the other side of the room stood the intricate mass of machinery, reaching well up into the open second story, that wafted passengers through the space that stretched from star to star.

An inn, he thought, a stopping place, a galactic crossroads.

He rolled up the chart and put it back into the desk. The record book he put away in its proper place among all the other record books upon the shelf.

He glanced at the galactic clock upon the wall and it was time to go.

He pushed the chair tight against the desk and shrugged into the jacket that hung upon the chair back. He picked the rifle off the supports that held it on the wall and then he faced the wall itself and said the single word that he had to say. The wall slid back silently and he stepped through it into the little shed with its sparse furnishings. Behind him the section of the wall slid back and there was nothing there to indicate it was anything but a solid wall.

Enoch stepped out of the shed and it was a beautiful late summer day. In a few weeks now, he thought, there'd be the signs of autumn and a strange chill in the air. The first goldenrods were blooming now and he'd noticed, just the day before, that some of the early asters down in the ancient fence row had started to show color.

He went around the corner of the house and headed toward the river, striding down the long deserted field that was overrun with hazel brush and occasional clumps of trees.

This was the Earth, he thought—a planet made for Man. But not for Man alone, for it was as well a planet for the fox and owl and weasel, for the snake, the katydid, the fish, for all the other teeming life that filled the air and earth and water. And not these natives alone, but for other beings that called other earths their home, other planets that far light-years distant were basically the same as Earth. For Ulysses and the Hazers and all the rest of them who could live upon this planet, if need be, if they wished, with no discomfort and no artificial aids.

Our horizons are so far, he thought, and we see so little of them. Even now, with flaming rockets striving from Canaveral to break the ancient bonds, we dream so little of them.

The ache was there, the ache that had been growing, the ache to tell all mankind those things that he had learned. Not so much the specific things, although there were some of them that mankind well could use, but the general things, the unspecific, central fact that there was intelligence throughout the universe, that Man was not alone, that if he only found the way he need never be alone again.

He went down across the field and through the strip of woods and came out on the great outthrust of rock that stood atop the cliff that faced the river. He stood there, as he had stood on thousands of other mornings, and stared out at the river, sweeping in majestic blue-and-silverness through the wooded bottom land.

Old, ancient water, he said, talking silently to the river, you have seen it happen—the mile-high faces of the glaciers that came and stayed and left, creeping back toward the pole inch by stubborn inch, carrying the melting water from those very glaciers in a flood that filled this valley with a tide such as now is never known; the mastodon and the sabertooth and the bear-sized beaver that ranged these olden hills and made the night clamorous with trumpeting and screaming; the silent little bands of men who trotted in the woods or clambered up the cliffs or paddled on your surface, woods-wise and water-wise, weak in body, strong in purpose, and persistent in a way no other thing ever was persistent, and just a little time ago that other breed of men who carried dreams within their skulls and cruelty in their hands and the awful sureness of an even greater purpose in their hearts. And before that, for this is ancient country beyond what is often found, the other kinds of life and the many turns of climate and the changes that came upon the Earth itself. And what think you of it? he asked the river. For yours is the memory and the perspective and the time and by now you should have the answers, or at least some of the answers.

As Man might have some of the answers had he lived for several million years—as he might have the answers several million years from this very summer morning if he still should be around.

I could help, thought Enoch. I could not give the answers, but I could help Man in his scramble after them. I could give him faith and hope and I could give purpose such as he has not had before.

But he knew he dare not do it.

Far below a hawk swung in lazy circles above the highway of the river. The air was so clear that Enoch imagined, if he strained his eyes a little, he could see every feather in those outspread wings.

There was almost a fairy quality to this place, he thought. The far look and the clear air and the feeling of detachment that touched almost on greatness of the spirit. As if this were a special place, one of those special places that each man must seek out for himself, and count himself as lucky if he ever found it, for there were those who sought and never found it. And worst of all, there were even those who never hunted for it.

He stood upon the rock and stared out across the river, watching the lazy hawk and the sweep of water and the green carpeting of trees, and his mind went up and out to those other places until his mind was dizzy with the thought of it. And then he called it home.

He turned slowly and went back down the rock and moved off among the trees, following the path he'd beaten through the years.

He considered going down the hill a way to look in on the patch of pink lady's-slippers, to see how they might be coming, to try to conjure up the beauty that would be his again in June, but decided that there'd be little point to it, for they were well hidden in an isolated place, and nothing could have harmed them. There had been a time, a hundred years ago, when they had bloomed on every hill and he had come trailing home with great armloads of them, which his mother had put in the great brown jug she had, and for a day or two the house had been filled with the heaviness of their rich perfume. But they were hard to come by now. The trampling of pastured cattle and flower-hunting humans had swept them from the hills.

Some other day, he told himself, some day before first frost, he would visit them again and satisfy himself that they'd be there in the spring.

He stopped a while to watch a squirrel as it frolicked in an oak. He squatted down to follow a snail which had crossed his path. He stopped beside a massive tree and examined the pattern of the moss that grew upon its trunk. And he traced the wanderings of a silent, flitting songbird as it fluttered tree to tree.

He followed the path out of the woods and along the edge of field until he came to the spring that bubbled from the hillside.

Sitting beside the spring was a woman and he recognized her as Lucy Fisher, the deaf-mute daughter of Hank Fisher, who lived down in the river bottoms.

He stopped and watched her and thought how full she was of grace and beauty, the natural grace and beauty of a primitive and lonely creature.

She was sitting by the spring and one hand was uplifted and she held in it, at the tips of long and sensitive fingers, something that glowed with color. Her head was held high, with a sharp look of alertness, and her body was straight and slender, and it also had that almost startled look of quiet alertness.

Enoch moved slowly forward and stopped not more than three feet behind her, and now he saw that the thing of color on her fingertips was a butterfly, one of those large gold and red butterflies that come with the end of summer. One wing of the insect stood erect and straight, but the other was bent and crumpled and had lost some of the dust that lent sparkle to the color.

She was, he saw, not actually holding the butterfly. It was standing on one fingertip, the one good wing fluttering very slightly every now and then to maintain its balance.

But he had been mistaken, he saw, in thinking that the second wing was injured, for now he could see that somehow it had been simply bent and distorted in some way. For now it was straightening slowly and the dust (if it ever had been gone) was back on it again, and it was standing up with the other wing.

He stepped around the girl so that she could see him and when she saw him there was no start of surprise. And that, he knew, would be quite natural, for she must be accustomed to it—someone coming up behind her and suddenly being there.

Her eyes were radiant and there was, he thought, a holy look upon her face, as if she had experienced some ecstasy of the soul. And he found himself wondering again, as he did each time he saw her, what it must be like for her, living in a world of two-way silence, unable to communicate. Perhaps not entirely unable to communicate, but at least barred from that free flow of communication which was the birthright of the human animal.

There had been, he knew, several attempts to establish her in a state school for the deaf, but each had been a failure. Once she'd run away and wandered days before being finally found and returned to her home. And on other occasions she had gone on disobedience strikes, refusing to co-operate in any of the teaching.

Watching her as she sat there with the butterfly, Enoch

thought he knew the reason. She had a world, he thought, a world of her very own, one to which she was accustomed and knew how to get along in. In that world she was no cripple, as she most surely would have been a cripple if she had been pushed, part way, into the normal human world.

What good to her the hand alphabet or the reading of the lips if they should take from her some strange inner serenity of spirit?

She was a creature of the woods and hills, of springtime flower and autumn flight of birds. She knew these things and lived with them and was, in some strange way, a specific part of them. She was one who dwelt apart in an old and lost apartment of the natural world. She occupied a place that Man long since had abandoned, if, in fact, he'd ever held it.

And there she sat, with the wild red and gold of the butterfly poised upon her finger, with the sense of alertness and expectancy and, perhaps, accomplishment shining on her face. She was alive, thought Enoch, as no other thing he knew had ever been alive.

The butterfly spread its wings and floated off her finger and went fluttering, unconcerned, unfrightened, up across the wild grass and the goldenrod of the field.

She pivoted to watch it until it disappeared near the top of the hill up which the old field climbed, then she turned to Enoch. She smiled and made a fluttery motion with her hands, like the fluttering of the red and golden wings, but there was something else in it, as well—a sense of happiness and an expression of well-being, as if she might be saying that the world was going fine.

If, Enoch thought, I could only teach her the pasimology of my galactic people—then we could talk, the two of us, almost as well as with the flow of words on the human tongue. Given the time, he thought, it might not be too hard, for there was a natural and a logical process to the galactic sign language that made it almost instinctive once one had caught the underlying principle.

Throughout the Earth as well, in the early days, there had been sign languages, and none so well developed as that one which obtained among the aborigines of North America, so that an Amerindian, no matter what his tongue, could express himself among many other tribes.

But even so the sign language of the Indian was, at best, a crutch that allowed a man to hobble when he couldn't run. Whereas that of the galaxy was in itself a language, adaptable to many different means and methods of expression. It had been developed through millennia, with many different peoples making contributions, and through the centuries it had been refined and shaken down and polished until today it was a communications tool that stood on its own merits.

There was need for such a tool, for the galaxy was Babel. Even the galactic science of pasimology, polished as it might be, could not surmount all the obstacles, could not guarantee, in certain cases, the basic minimum of communication. For not only were there millions of tongues, but those other languages as well which could not operate on the principle of sound because the races were incapable of sound. And even sound itself failed of efficiency when the race talked in ultrasonics others could not hear. There was telepathy, of course, but for every telepath there were a thousand races that had telepathic blocks. There were many who got along on sign languages alone and others who could communicate only by a written or pictographic system, including some who carried chemical blackboards built into their bodies. And there was that sightless, deaf, and speechless race from the mystery stars of the far side of the galaxy who used what was perhaps the most complicated of all the galactic languages—a code of signals routed along their nervous systems.

Enoch had been at the job almost a century, and even so, he thought, with the aid of the universal sign language and the semantic translator, which was little more than a pitiful (although complicated) mechanical contrivance, he still was hard put at times to know what many of them said.

Lucy Fisher picked up a cup that was standing by her side— a cup fashioned of a strip of folded birch bark—and dipped it in the spring. She held it out to Enoch and he stepped close to take it, kneeling down to drink from it. It was not entirely water-tight, and water ran from it down across his arm, wetting the cuff of shirt and jacket.

He finished drinking and handed back the cup. She took it in one hand and reached out the other, to brush across his fore-head with the tip of gentle fingers in what she might have thought of as a benediction.

He did not speak to her. Long ago he had ceased talking to her, sensing that the movement of his mouth, making sounds she could not hear, might be embarrassing.

Instead he put out a hand and laid his broad palm against her cheek, holding it there for a reassuring moment as a gesture of affection. Then he got to his feet and stood staring down at her and for a moment their eyes looked into the other's eyes and then turned away.

He crossed the little stream that ran down from the spring and took the trail that led from the forest's edge across the field, heading for the ridge. Halfway up the slope, he turned around and saw that she was watching him. He held up his hand in a gesture of farewell and her hand gestured in reply.

It had been, he recalled, twelve years or more ago that he first had seen her, a little fairy person of ten years or so, a wild thing running in the woods. They had become friends, he re-called, only after a long time, although he saw her often, for she roamed the hills and valley as if they were a playground for her—which, of course, they were.

Through the years he had watched her grow and had often met her on his daily walks, and between the two of them had grown up an understanding of the lonely and the outcast, but understanding based on something more than that—on the fact that each had a world that was their own and worlds that had given them an insight into something that others seldom saw. Not that either, Enoch thought, ever told the other, or tried to tell the other, of these private worlds, but the fact of these private worlds was there, in the consciousness of each, providing a firm foundation for the building of a friendship.

He recalled the day he'd found her at the place where the pink lady's-slippers grew, just kneeling there and looking at them, not picking any of them, and how he'd stopped beside her and been pleased she had not moved to pick them, knowing that in the sight of them, the two, he and she, had found a joy and a beauty that was beyond possession.

He reached the ridgetop and turned down the grass-grown road that led down to the mailbox.

And he'd not been mistaken back there, he told himself, no matter how it may have seemed on second look. The butterfly's wing had been torn and crumpled and drab from the lack of dust. It had been a crippled thing and then it had been whole again and had flown away.

8

Winslowe Grant was on time.

Enoch, as he reached the mailbox, sighted the dust raised by his old jalopy as it galloped along the ridge. It had been a dusty year, he thought, as he stood beside the box. There had been little rain and the crops had suffered. Although, to tell the truth, there were few crops on the ridge these days. There had been a time when comfortable small farms had existed, almost cheek by jowl, all along the road, with the barns all red and the houses white. But now most of the farms had been abandoned and the houses and the barns were no longer red or white, but gray and weathered wood, with all the paint peeled off and the ridgepoles sagging and the people gone.

It would not be long before Winslowe would arrive and Enoch settled down to wait. The mailman might be stopping at the Fisher box, just around the bend, although the Fishers, as a rule, got but little mail, mostly just the advertising sheets and other junk that was mailed out indiscriminately to the rural boxholders. Not that it mattered to the Fishers, for sometimes days went by in which they did not pick up their mail. If it were not for Lucy, they perhaps would never get it, for it was mostly Lucy who thought to pick it up.

The Fishers were, for a fact, Enoch told himself, a truly shiftless outfit. Their house and all the buildings were ready to fall in upon themselves and they raised a grubby patch of corn that was drowned out, more often than not, by a flood rise of the river. They mowed some hay off a bottom meadow and they had a couple of raw-boned horses and a half-dozen scrawny cows and a flock of chickens. They had an old clunk of a car and a still hidden out somewhere in the river bottoms and they hunted and fished and trapped and were generally no-account. Although, when one considered it, they were not bad neighbors. They tended to their business and never bothered anyone except that periodically they went around, the whole tribe of them, distributing pamphlets and tracts through the neighborhood for some obscure fundamentalist sect that Ma Fisher had become a member of at a tent revival meeting down in Millville several years before.

Winslowe didn't stop at the Fisher box, but came boiling around the bend in a cloud of dust. He braked the panting machine to a halt and turned off the engine.

"Let her cool a while," he said.

The block crackled as it started giving up its heat.

"You made good time today," said Enoch.

"Lots of people didn't have any mail today," said Winslowe. "Just went sailing past their boxes."

He dipped into the pouch on the seat beside him and brought

out a bundle tied together with a bit of string for Enoch—several daily papers and two journals.

"You get a lot of stuff," said Winslowe, "but hardly ever letters."

"There is no one left," said Enoch, "who would want to write to me."

"But," said Winslowe, "you got a letter this time."

Enoch looked, unable to conceal surprise, and could see the end of an envelope peeping from between the journals.

"A personal letter," said Winslowe, almost smacking his lips. "Not one of them advertising ones. Nor a business one."

Enoch tucked the bundle underneath his arm, beside the rifle stock.

"Probably won't amount to much," he said.

"Maybe not," said Winslowe, a sly glitter in his eyes.

He pulled a pipe and pouch from his pocket and slowly filled the pipe. The engine block continued its crackling and popping. The sun beat down out of a cloudless sky. The vegetation alongside the road was coated with dust and an acrid smell rose from it.

"Hear that ginseng fellow is back again," said Winslowe, conversationally, but unable to keep out a conspiratorial tone. "Been gone for three, four days."

"Maybe off to sell his sang."

"You ask me," the mailman said, "he ain't hunting sang. He's hunting something else."

"Been at it," Enoch said, "for a right smart time."

"First of all," said Winslowe, "there's barely any market for the stuff and even if there was, there isn't any sang. Used to be a good market years ago. Chinese used it for medicine, I guess. But now there ain't no trade with China. I remember when I was a boy we used to go hunting it. Not easy to find, even then. But most days a man could locate a little of it."

He leaned back in the seat, puffing serenely at his pipe.

"Funny goings on," he said.

"I never saw the man," said Enoch.

"Sneaking through the woods," said Winslowe. "Digging up different kinds of plants. Got the idea myself he maybe is a sort of magic-man. Getting stuff to make up charms and such. Spends a lot of his time yarning with the Fisher tribe and drinking up their likker. You don't hear much of it these days, but I still hold with magic. Lots of things science can't explain. You take that Fisher girl, the dummy, she can charm off warts."

"So I've heard," said Enoch.

And more than that, he thought. She can fix a butterfly.

Winslowe hunched forward in his seat.

"Almost forgot," he said. "I have something else for you."

He lifted a brown paper parcel from the floor and handed it to Enoch.

"This ain't mail," he said. "It's something that I made for you."

"Why, thank you," Enoch said, taking it from him.

"Go ahead," Winslowe said, "and open it up."

Enoch hesitated.

"Ah, hell," said Winslowe, "don't be bashful."

Enoch tore off the paper and there it was, a full-figure wood carving of himself. It was in a blond, honey-colored wood and some twelve inches tall. It shone like golden crystal in the sun. He was walking, with his rifle tucked beneath his arm and a wind was blowing, for he was leaning slightly into it and there were wind-flutter ripples on his jacket and his trousers.

Enoch gasped, then stood staring at it.

"Wins," he said, "that's the most beautiful piece of work I have ever seen."

"Did it," said the mailman, "out of that piece of wood you gave me last winter. Best piece of whittling stuff I ever ran across. Hard and without hardly any grain. No danger of splitting or of nicking or of shredding. When you make a cut, you make it where you want to and it stays the way you cut it. And it takes polish as you cut. Just rub it up a little is all you need to do."

"You don't know," said Enoch, "how much this means to me."

"Over the years," the mailman told him, "you've given me an awful lot of wood. Different kinds of wood no one's ever seen before. All of it top-grade stuff and beautiful. It was time I was carving something for you."

"And you," said Enoch, "have done a lot for me. Lugging things from town."

"Enoch," Winslowe said, "I like you. I don't know what you are and I ain't about to ask, but anyhow I like you."

"I wish that I could tell you what I am," said Enoch.

"Well," said Winslowe, moving over to plant himself behind the wheel, "it don't matter much what any of us are, just so we get along with one another. If some of the nations would only take a lesson from some small neighborhood like ours—a lesson in how to get along—the world would be a whole lot better."

Enoch nodded gravely. "It doesn't look too good, does it?"

"It sure don't," said the mailman, starting up the car.

Enoch stood and watched the car move off, down the hill, building up its cloud of dust as it moved along.

Then he looked again at the wooden statuette of himself.

It was as if the wooden figure were walking on a hilltop, naked to the full force of the wind and bent against the gale.

Why? He wondered. What was it the mailman had seen in him to portray him as walking in the wind?

9

He laid the rifle and the mail upon a patch of dusty grass and carefully rewrapped the statuette in the piece of paper. He'd put it, he decided, either on the mantelpiece or, perhaps better yet, on the coffee table that stood beside his favorite chair in the corner by the desk. He wanted it, he admitted to himself, with some quiet embarrassment, where it was close at hand, where he could look at it or pick it up any time he wished. And he wondered at the deep, heart-warming, soul-satisfying pleasure that he got from the mailman's gift.

It was not, he knew, because he was seldom given gifts. Scarcely a week went past that the alien travelers did not leave several with him. The house was cluttered and there was a wall of shelves down in the cavernous basement that were crammed with the stuff that had been given him. Perhaps it was, he told himself, because this was a gift from Earth, from one of his own kind.

He tucked the wrapped statuette beneath his arm and, picking up the rifle and the mail, headed back for home, following the brush-grown trail that once had been the wagon road leading to the farm.

Grass had grown into thick turf between the ancient ruts, which had been cut so deep into the clay by the iron tires of the old-time wagons that they still were no more than bare, impacted earth in which no plant as yet had gained a root-hold. But on each side the clumps of brush, creeping up the field from the forest's edge, grew man-high or better, so that now one moved down an aisle of green.

But at certain points, quite unexplainably—perhaps due to the character of the soil or to the mere vagaries of nature—the growth of brush had faltered, and here were vistas where one might look out from the ridgetop across the river valley.

It was from one of these vantage points that Enoch caught the flash from a clump of trees at the edge of the old field, not too far from the spring where he had found Lucy.

He frowned as he saw the flash and stood quietly on the path, waiting for its repetition. But it did not come again.

It was one of the watchers, he knew, using a pair of binoculars to keep watch upon the station. The flash he had seen had been the reflection of the sun upon the glasses.

Who were they? he wondered. And why should they be watching? It had been going on for some time now but, strangely, there had been nothing but the watching. There had been no interference. No one had attempted to approach him, and such approach, he realized, could have been quite simple and quite natural. If they—whoever they might be—had wished to talk with him, a very casual meeting could have been arranged during any one of his morning walks.

But apparently as yet they did not wish to talk.

What, then, he wondered, did they wish to do? Keep track of him, perhaps. And in that regard, he thought, with a wry inner twinge of humor, they could have become acquainted with the pattern of his living in their first ten days of watching.

Or perhaps they might be waiting for some happening that would provide them with a clue to what he might be doing. And in that direction there lay nothing but certain disappointment. They could watch for a thousand years and gain no hint of it.

He turned from the vista and went plodding up the road, worried and puzzled by his knowledge of the watchers.

Perhaps, he thought, they had not attempted to contact him because of certain stories that might be told about him. Stories that no one, not even Winslowe, would pass on to him. What kind of stories, he wondered, might the neighborhood by now have been able to fabricate about him—fabulous folk tales to be told in bated breath about the chimney corner?

It might be well, he thought, that he did not know the stories, although it would seem almost a certainty that they would exist. And it also might be as well that the watchers had not attempted contact with him. For so long as there was no contact, he still was fairly safe. So long as there were no questions, there need not be any answers.

Are you really, they would ask, that same Enoch Wallace

who marched off in 1861 to fight for old Abe Lincoln? And there was one answer to that, there could only be one answer. Yes, he'd have to say, I am that same man.

And of all the questions they might ask him that would be the only one of all he could answer truthfully. For all the others there would necessarily be silence or evasion.

They would ask how come that he had not aged—how he could stay young when all mankind grew old. And he could not tell them that he did not age inside the station, that he only aged when he stepped out of it, that he aged an hour each day on his daily walks, that he might age an hour or so working in his garden, that he could age for fifteen minutes sitting on the steps to watch a lovely sunset. But that when he went back indoors again the aging process was completely canceled out.

He could not tell them that. And there was much else that he could not tell them. There might come a time, he knew, if they once contacted him, that he'd have to flee the questions and cut himself entirely from the world, remaining isolated within the station's walls.

Such a course would constitute no hardship physically, for he could live within the station without any inconvenience. He would want for nothing, for the aliens would supply everything he needed to remain alive and well. He had bought human food at times, having Winslowe purchase it and haul it out from town, but only because he felt a craving for the food of his own planet, in particular those simple foods of his childhood and his campaigning days.

And, he told himself, even these foods might well be supplied by the process of duplication. A slab of bacon or a dozen eggs could be sent to another station and remain there as a master pattern for the pattern impulses, being sent to him on order as he needed them.

But there was one thing the aliens could not provide—the human contacts he'd maintained through Winslowe and the mail. Once shut inside the station, he'd be cut off completely from the world he knew, for the newspapers and the magazines were his only contact. The operation of a radio in the station was made impossible by the interference set up by the installations.

He would not know what was happening in the world, would know no longer how the outside might be going. His chart would suffer from this and would become largely useless; although, he told himself, it was nearly useless now, since he could not be certain of the correct usage of the factors.

But aside from all of this, he would miss this little outside world that he had grown to know so well, this little corner of the world encompassed by his walks. It was the walks, he thought, more than anything, perhaps, that had kept him human and a citizen of Earth.

He wondered how important it might be that he remain, intellectually and emotionally, a citizen of Earth and a member of the human race. There was, he thought, perhaps no reason that he should. With the cosmopolitanism of the galaxy at his fingertips, it might even be provincial of him to be so intent upon his continuing identification with the old home planet. He might be losing something by this provincialism.

But it was not in himself, he knew, to turn his back on Earth. It was a place he loved too well—loving it more, most likely, than those other humans who had not caught his glimpse of far and unguessed worlds. A man, he told himself, must belong to something, must have some loyalty and some identity. The galaxy was too big a place for any being to stand naked and alone.

A lark sailed out of a grassy plot and soared high into the sky, and seeing it, he waited for the trill of liquid song to spray out of its throat and drip out of the blue. But there was no song, as there would have been in spring.

He plodded down the road and now, ahead of him, he saw the starkness of the station, reared upon its ridge.

Funny, he thought, that he should think of it as station rather than as home, but it had been a station longer than it had been a home.

There was about it, he saw, a sort of ugly solidness, as if it might have planted itself upon that ridgetop and meant to stay forever.

It would stay, of course, if one wanted it, as long as one wanted it. For there was nothing that could touch it.

Even should he be forced some day to remain within its walls, the station still would stand against all of mankind's watching, all of mankind's prying. They could not chip it and they could not gouge it and they could not break it down. There was nothing they could do. All his watching, all his speculating, all his analyzing, would gain Man nothing beyond the knowledge that a highly unusual building existed on that ridgetop. For it could survive anything except a thermonuclear explosion—and maybe even that.

He walked into the yard and turned around to look back toward the clump of trees from which the flash had come, but there was nothing now to indicate that anyone was there.

10

Inside the station, the message machine was whistling plaintively.

Enoch hung up his gun, dropped the mail and statuette upon his desk and strode across the room to the whistling machine. He pushed the button and punched the lever and the whistling stopped.

Upon the message plate he read:

NO. 406,302 TO STATION 18327. WILL ARRIVE EARLY EVENING YOUR TIME. HAVE THE COFFEE HOT. ULYSSES.

Enoch grinned. Ulysses and his coffee! He was the only one of the aliens who had ever liked any of Earth's foods or drinks. There had been others who had tried them, but not more than once or twice.

Funny about Ulysses, he thought. They had liked each other from the very first, from that afternoon of the thunderstorm when they had been sitting on the steps and the mask of human form had peeled off the alien's face.

It had been a grisly face, graceless and repulsive. The face, Enoch had thought, of a cruel clown. Wondering, even as he thought it, what had put that particular phrase into his head, for clowns were never cruel. But here was one that could be— the colored patchwork of the face, the hard, tight set of jaw, the thin slash of the mouth.

Then he saw the eyes and they canceled all the rest. They were large and had a softness and the light of understanding in them, and they reached out to him, as another being might hold out its hands in friendship.

The rain had come hissing up the land to thrum across the machine-shed roof, and then it was upon them, slanting sheets of rain that hammered angrily at the dust which lay across the yard, while surprised, bedraggled chickens ran frantically for cover.

Enoch sprang to his feet and grasped the other's arm, pulling him to the shelter of the porch.

They stood facing one another, and Ulysses had reached up and pulled the split and loosened mask away, revealing a bullet head without a hair upon it—and the painted face. A face like a wild and rampaging Indian, painted for the warpath, except that here and there were touches of the clown, as if the entire painting job had been meant to point up the inconsistent grotesqueries of war. But even as he stared, Enoch knew it was not paint, but the natural coloration of this thing which had come from somewhere among the stars.

Whatever other doubt there was, or whatever wonder, Enoch

had no doubt at all that this strange being was not of the Earth. For it was not human. It might be in human form, with a pair of arms and legs, with a head and face. But there was about it an essence of inhumanity, almost a negation of humanity.

In olden days, perhaps, he thought, it might have been a demon, but the days were past (although, in some areas of the country, not entirely past) when one believed in demons or in ghosts or in any of the others of that ghastly tribe which, in man's imagination, once had walked the Earth.

From the stars, he'd said. And perhaps he was. Although it made no sense. It was nothing one ever had imagined even in the purest fantasy. There was nothing to grab hold of, nothing to hang on to. There was no yardstick for it and there were no rules. And it left a sort of blank spot in one's thinking that might fill in, come time, but now was no more than a tunnel of great wonder that went on and on forever.

"Take your time," the alien said. "I know it is not easy. And I do not know of a thing that I can do to make it easier. There is, after all, no way for me to prove I am from the stars."

"But you talk so well."

"In your tongue, you mean. It was not too difficult. If you only knew of all the languages in the galaxy, you would realize how little difficult. Your language is not hard. It is a basic one and there are many concepts with which it need not deal."

And, Enoch conceded, that could be true enough.

"If you wish," the alien said, "I can walk off somewhere for a day or two. Give you time to think. Then I could come back. You'd have thought it out by then."

Enoch smiled, woodenly, and the smile had an unnatural feel upon his face.

"That would give me time," he said, "to spread alarm throughout the countryside. There might be an ambush waiting for you."

The alien shook its head. "I am sure you wouldn't do it. I would take the chance. If you want me to . . ."

"No," said Enoch, so calmly he surprised himself. "No, when

you have a thing to face, you face it. I learned that in the war."

"You'll do," the alien said. "You will do all right. I did not misjudge you and it makes me proud."

"Misjudge me?"

"You do not think I just came walking in here cold? I know about you, Enoch. Almost as much, perhaps, as you know about yourself. Probably even more."

"You know my name?"

"Of course I do."

"Well, that is fine," said Enoch. "And what about your own?"

"I am seized with great embarrassment," the alien told him. "For I have no name as such. Identification, surely, that fits the purpose of my race, but nothing that the tongue can form."

Suddenly, for no reason, Enoch remembered that slouchy figure perching on the top rail of a fence, with a stick in one hand and a jackknife in the other, whittling placidly while the cannon balls whistled overhead and less than half a mile away the muskets snarled and crackled in the billowing powder smoke that rose above the line.

"Then you need a name to call you by," he said, "and it shall be Ulysses. I need to call you something."

"It is agreeable," said that strange one. "But might one ask why the name Ulysses?"

"Because it is the name," said Enoch, "of a great man of my race."

It was a crazy thing, of course. For there was no resemblance between the two of them—that slouchy Union general whittling as he perched upon the fence and this other who stood upon the porch.

"I am glad you chose it," said this Ulysses, standing on the porch. "To my hearing it has a dignified and noble sound and, between the two of us, I shall be glad to bear it. And I shall call you Enoch, as friends of the first names, for the two of us shall work together for many of your years."

It was beginning to come straight now and the thought was

staggering. Perhaps it was as well, Enoch told himself, that it had waited for a while, that he had been so dazed it had not come on him all at once.

"Perhaps," said Enoch, fighting back the realization that was crowding in on him, crowding in too fast, "I could offer you some victuals. I could cook up some coffee . . ."

"Coffee," said Ulysses, smacking his thin lips. "Do you have the coffee?"

"I'll make a big pot of it. I'll break in an egg so it will settle clear . . ."

"Delectable," Ulysses said. "Of all the drinks that I have drank on all the planets I have visited, the coffee is the best."

They went into the kitchen and Enoch stirred up the coals in the kitchen range and then put in new wood. He took the coffeepot over to the sink and ladled in some water from the water pail and put it on to boil. He went into the pantry to get some eggs and down into the cellar to bring up the ham.

Ulysses sat stiffly in a kitchen chair and watched him as he worked.

"You eat ham and eggs?" asked Enoch.

"I eat anything," Ulysses said. "My race is most adaptable. That is the reason I was sent to this planet as a—what do you call it?—a looker-out, perhaps."

"A scout," suggested Enoch.

"That is it, a scout."

He was an easy thing to talk with, Enoch told himself—almost like another person, although, God knows, he looked little like a person. He looked, instead, like some outrageous caricature of a human being.

"You have lived here, in this house," Ulysses said, "for a long, long time. You feel affection for it."

"It has been my home," said Enoch, "since the day that I was born. I was gone from it for almost four years, but it was always home."

"I'll be glad," Ulysses told him, "to be getting home again

myself. I've been away too long. On a mission such as this one, it always is too long."

Enoch put down the knife he had been using to cut a slice of ham and sat down heavily in a chair. He stared at Ulysses, across the table from him.

"You?" he asked. "You are going home?"

"Why, of course," Ulysses told him. "Now that my job is nearly done. I have got a home. Did you think I hadn't?"

"I don't know," said Enoch weakly. "I had never thought of it."

And that was it, he knew. It had not occurred to him to connect a being such as this with a thing like home. For it was only human beings that had a place called home.

"Some day," Ulysses said, "I shall tell you about my home. Some day you may even visit me."

"Out among the stars," said Enoch.

"It seems strange to you now," Ulysses said. "It will take a while to get used to the idea. But as you come to know us—all of us—you will understand. And I hope you like us. We are not bad people, really. Not any of the many different kinds of us."

The stars, Enoch told himself, were out there in the loneliness of space and how far they were he could not even guess, nor what they were nor why. Another world, he thought—no, that was wrong—many other worlds. There were people there, perhaps many other people; a different kind of people, probably, for every different star. And one of them sat here in this very kitchen, waiting for the coffeepot to boil, for the ham and eggs to fry.

"But why?" he asked. "But why?"

"Because," Ulysses said, "we are a traveling people. We need a travel station here. We want to turn this house into a station and you to keep the station."

"This house?"

"We could not build a station, for then we'd have people asking who was building it and what it might be for. So we are forced to use an existing structure and change it for our needs. But the inside only. We leave the outside as it is, in appearance, that is. For there must be no questions asked. There must be . . ."

"But traveling . . ."

"From star to star," Ulysses said. "Quicker than the thought of it. Faster than a wink. There is what you would call machinery, but it is not machinery—not the same as the machinery you think of."

"You must excuse me," Enoch said, confused. "It seems so impossible."

"You remember when the railroad came to Millville?"

"Yes, I can remember that. I was just a kid."

"Then think of it this way. This is just another railroad and the Earth is just another town and this house will be the station for this new and different railroad. The only difference is that no one on Earth but you will know the railroad's here. For it will be no more than a resting and a switching point. No one on the Earth can buy a ticket to travel on the railroad."

Put that way, of course, it had a simple sound, but it was, Enoch sensed, very far from simple.

"Railroad cars in space?" he asked.

"Not railroad cars," Ulysses told him. "It is something else. I do not know how to begin to tell you . . ."

"Perhaps you should pick someone else. Someone who would understand."

"There is no one on this planet who could remotely understand. No, Enoch, we'll do with you as well as anyone. In many ways, much better than with anyone."

"But . . ."

"What is it, Enoch?"

"Nothing," Enoch said.

For he remembered now how he had been sitting on the steps thinking how he was alone and about a new beginning, knowing that he could not escape a new beginning, that he must start from scratch and build his life anew.

And here, suddenly, was that new beginning—more wondrous and fearsome than anything he could have dreamed even in an insane moment.

11

Enoch filed the message and sent his confirmation:

NO. 406302 RECEIVED. COFFEE ON THE FIRE. ENOCH.

Clearing the machine, he walked over to the No. 3 liquid tank he'd prepared before he left. He checked the temperature and the level of the solution and made certain once again that the tank was securely positioned in relation to the materializer.

From there he went to the other materializer, the official and emergency materializer, positioned in the corner, and checked it over closely. It was all right, as usual. It always was all right, but before each of Ulysses's visits he never failed to check it. There was nothing he could have done about it had there been something wrong other than send an urgent message to Galactic Central. In which case someone would have come in on the regular materializer and put it into shape.

For the official and emergency materializer was exactly what its name implied. It was used only for official visits by personnel of Galactic Center or for possible emergencies and its operation was entirely outside that of the local station.

Ulysses, as an inspector for this and several other stations, could have used the official materializer at any time he wished without prior notice. But in all the years that he had been coming to the station he had never failed, Enoch remembered with a touch of pride, to message that he was coming. It was, he knew, a courtesy which all the other stations on the great galactic network might not be accorded, although there were some of them which might be given equal treatment.

Tonight, he thought, he probably should tell Ulysses about the watch that had been put upon the station. Perhaps he should have told him earlier, but he had been reluctant to admit that the human race might prove to be a problem to the galactic installation.

It was a hopeless thing, he thought, this obsession of his to present the people of the Earth as good and reasonable. For in many ways they were neither good nor reasonable; perhaps because they had not as yet entirely grown up. They were smart and quick and at times compassionate and even understanding, but they failed lamentably in many other ways.

But if they had the chance, Enoch told himself, if they ever got a break, if they only could be told what was out in space, then they'd get a grip upon themselves and they would measure up and then, in the course of time, would be admitted into the great cofraternity of the people of the stars.

Once admitted, they would prove their worth and would pull their weight, for they were still a young race and full of energy—at times, maybe, too much energy.

Enoch shook his head and went across the room to sit down at his desk. Drawing the bundle of mail in front of him, he slid it out of the string which Winslowe had used to tie it all together.

There were the daily papers, a news weekly, two journals—*Nature* and *Science*—and the letter.

He pushed the papers and the journals to one side and picked up the letter. It was, he saw, an air mail sheet and was postmarked London and the return address bore a name that was unfamiliar to him. He puzzled as to why an unknown person should be writing him from London. Although, he reminded himself, anyone who wrote from London, or indeed from anywhere, would be an unknown person. He knew no one in London nor elsewhere in the world.

He slit the air sheet open and spread it out on the desk in front of him, pulling the desk lamp close so the light would fall upon the writing.

Dear sir [he read], *I would suspect I am unknown to you. I am one of the several editors of the British journal,* Nature, *to which you have been a subscriber for these many years. I do not use the journal's letterhead because this letter is personal and unofficial and perhaps not even in the best of taste.*

You are, it may interest you to know, our eldest subscriber. We have had you on our mailing lists for more than eighty years.

While I am aware that it is no appropriate concern of mine, I have wondered if you, yourself, have subscribed to our publication for this length of time, or if it might be possible that your father or someone close to you may have been the original subscriber and you simply have allowed the subscription to continue in his name.

My interest undoubtedly constitutes an unwarranted and inexcusable curiosity and if you, sir, choose to ignore the query it is entirely within your rights and proper that you do so. But if you should not mind replying, an answer would be appreciated.

I can only say in my own defense that I have been associated for so long with our publication that I feel a certain sense of pride that someone has found it worth the having for more than eighty years. I doubt that many publications can boast such long time interest on the part of any man.

May I assure, you, sir, of my utmost respect.

Sincerely yours.

And then the signature.

Enoch shoved the letter from him.

And there it was again, he told himself. Here was another

watcher, although discreet and most polite and unlikely to cause trouble.

But someone else who had taken notice, who had felt a twinge of wonder at the same man subscribing to a magazine for more than eighty years.

As the years went on, there would be more and more. It was not only the watchers encamped outside the station with whom he must concern himself, but those potential others. A man could be as self-effacing as he well could manage and still he could not hide. Soon or late the world would catch up with him and would come crowding around his door, agog to know why he might be hiding.

It was useless, he knew, to hope for much further time. The world was closing in.

Why can't they leave me alone? he thought. If he only could explain how the situation stood, they might leave him alone. But he couldn't explain to them. And even if he could, there would be some of them who'd still come crowding in.

Across the room the materializer beeped for attention and Enoch swung around.

The Thuban had arrived. He was in the tank, a shadowy globular blob of substance, and above him, riding sluggishly in the solution, was a cube of something.

Luggage, Enoch wondered. But the message had said there would be no luggage.

Even as he hurried across the room, the clicking came to him —the Thuban talking to him.

"Presentation to you," said the clicking. "Deceased vegetation."

Enoch peered at the cube floating in the liquid.

"Take him," clicked the Thuban. "Bring him for you."

Fumblingly, Enoch clicked out his answer, using tapping fingers against the glass side of the tank: "I thank you, gracious one." Wondering as he did it, if he were using the proper form of address to this blob of matter. A man, he told himself, could get terribly tangled up on that particular point of etiquette.

There were some of these beings that one addressed in flowery language (and even in those cases, the floweriness would vary) and others that one talked with in the simplest, bluntest terms.

He reached into the tank and lifted out the cube and he saw that it was a block of heavy wood, black as ebony and so close-grained it looked very much like stone. He chuckled inwardly, thinking how, in listening to Winslowe, he had grown to be an expert in the judging of artistic wood.

He put the wood upon the floor and turned back to the tank.

"Would you mind," clicked the Thuban, "revealing what you do with him? To us, very useless stuff."

Enoch hesitated, searching desperately through his memory. What, he wondered, was the code for "carve?"

"Well?" the Thuban asked.

"You must pardon me, gracious one. I do not use this language often. I am not proficient."

"Drop, please, the 'gracious one.' I am a common being."

"Shape it," Enoch tapped. "Into another form. Are you a visual being? Then I show you one."

"Not visual," said the Thuban. "Many other things, not visual."

It had been a globe when it had arrived and now it was beginning to flatten out.

"You," the Thuban clicked, "are a biped being."

"That is what I am."

"Your planet. It is a solid planet?"

Solid? Enoch wondered. Oh, yes, solid as opposed to liquid.

"One-quarter solid," he tapped. "The rest of it is liquid."

"Mine almost all liquid. Only little solid. Very restful world."

"One thing I want to ask you," Enoch tapped.

"Ask," the creature said.

"You are a mathematician. All you folks, I mean."

"Yes," the creature said. "Excellent recreation. Occupies the mind."

"You mean you do not use it?"

"Oh, yes, once use it. But no need for use any more. Got all we need to use, very long ago. Recreation now."

"I have heard of your system of numerical notation."

"Very different," clicked the Thuban. "Very better concept."

"You can tell me of it?"

"You know notation system used by people of Polaris VII?"

"No, I don't," tapped Enoch.

"Then no use to tell you of our own. Must know Polaris first."

So that was that, thought Enoch. He might have known. There was so much knowledge in the galaxy and he knew so little of it, understood so little of the little that he knew.

There were men on Earth who could make sense of it. Men who would give anything short of their very lives to know the little that he knew, and could put it all to use.

Out among the stars lay a massive body of knowledge, some of it an extension of what mankind knew, some of it concerning matters which Man had not yet suspected, and used in ways and for purposes that Man had not as yet imagined. And never might imagine, if left on his own.

Another hundred years, thought Enoch. How much would he learn in another hundred years? In another thousand?

"I rest now," said the Thuban. "Nice to talk with you."

12

Enoch turned from the tank and picked up the block of wood. A little puddle of liquid had drained off it and lay glistening on the floor.

He carried the block across the room to one of the windows and examined it. It was heavy and black and close-grained and at one corner of it a bit of bark remained. It had been sawed.

Someone had cut it into a size that would fit the tank where the Thuban rested.

He recalled an article he had read in one of the daily papers just a day or two before in which a scientist had contended that no great intelligence ever could develop on a liquid world.

But that scientist was wrong, for the Thuban race had so developed and there were other liquid worlds which were members of the galactic cofraternity. There were a lot of things, he told himself, that Man would have to unlearn, as well as things to learn, if he ever should become aware of the galactic culture.

The limitation of the speed of light, for one thing.

For if nothing moved faster than the speed of light, then the galactic transport system would be impossible.

But one should not censure Man, he reminded himself, for setting the speed of light as a basic limitation. Observations were all that Man—or anyone, for that matter—could use as data upon which to base his premises. And since human science had so far found nothing which consistently moved faster than the speed of light, then the assumption must be valid that nothing could or did consistently move faster. But valid as an assumption only and no more than that.

For the impulse patterns which carried creatures star to star were almost instantaneous, no matter what the distance.

He stood and thought about it and it still was hard, he admitted to himself, for a person to believe.

Moments ago the creature in the tank had rested in another tank in another station and the materializer had built up a pattern of it—not only of its body, but of its very vital force, the thing that gave it life. Then the impulse pattern had moved across the gulfs of space almost instantaneously to the receiver of this station, where the pattern had been used to duplicate the body and the mind and memory and the life of that creature now lying dead many light years distant. And in the tank the new body and the new mind and memory and life had taken almost instant form—an entirely new being, but exactly like the old one, so that the identity continued and the consciousness (the very thought no more than momentarily interrupted), so that to all intent and purpose the being was the same.

There were limitations to the impulse patterns, but this had nothing to do with speed, for the impulses could cross the entire galaxy with but little lag in time. But under certain conditions the patterns tended to break down and this was why there must be many stations—many thousands of them. Clouds of dust or gas or areas of high ionization seemed to disrupt the patterns and in those sectors of the galaxy where these conditions were encountered, the distance jumps between the stations were considerably cut down to keep the pattern true. There were areas that had to be detoured because of high concentrations of the distorting gas and dust.

Enoch wondered how many dead bodies of the creature that now rested in the tank had been left behind at other stations in the course of the journey it was making—as this body in a few hours' time would lie dead within this tank when the creature's pattern was sent out again, riding on the impulse waves.

A long trail of dead, he thought, left across the stars, each to be destroyed by a wash of acid and flushed into deep-lying tanks, but with the creature itself going on and on until it reached its final destination to carry out the purpose of its journey.

And those purposes, Enoch wondered—the many purposes of the many creatures who passed through the stations scattered wide in space? There had been certain instances when, chatting with the travelers, they had told their purpose, but with the most of them he never learned the purpose—nor had he any right to learn it. For he was the keeper only.

Mine host, he thought, although not every time, for there were many creatures that had no use for hosts. But the man, at any rate, who watched over the operation of the station and who kept it going, who made ready for the travelers and who sent them on their way again when that time should come.

And who performed the little tasks and courtesies of which they might stand in need.

He looked at the block of wood and thought how pleased Winslowe would be with it. It was very seldom that one came upon a wood that was as black or fine-grained as this.

What would Winslowe think, he wondered, if he could only know that the statuettes he carved were made of woods that had grown on unknown planets many light years distant. Winslowe, he knew, must have wondered many times where the wood came from and how his friend could have gotten it. But he had never asked. And he knew as well, of course, that there was something very strange about this man who came out to the mailbox every day to meet him. But he had never asked that, either.

And that was friendship, Enoch told himself.

This wood, too, that he held in his hands, was another evidence of friendship—the friendship of the stars for a very humble keeper of a remote and backwoods station stuck out in one of the spiral arms, far from the center of the galaxy.

The word had spread, apparently, through the years and throughout space, that this certain keeper was a collector of exotic woods—and so the woods came in. Not only from those races he thought of as his friends, but from total strangers, like the blob that now rested in the tank.

He put the wood down on a table top and went to the refrigerator. From it he took a slab of aged cheese that Winslowe had bought for him several days ago, and a small package of fruit that a traveler from Sirrah X had brought the day before.

"Analyzed," it had told him, "and you can eat it without hurt. It will play no trouble with your metabolism. You've had it before, perhaps? So you haven't. I am sorry. It is most delicious. Next time, you like it, I shall bring you more."

From the cupboard beside the refrigerator he took out a small, flat loaf of bread, part of the ration regularly provided him by Galactic Central. Made of a cereal unlike any known on

Earth, it had a distinctly nutty flavor with the faintest hint of some alien spice.

He put the food on what he called the kitchen table, although there was no kitchen. Then he put the coffee maker on the stove and went back to his desk.

The letter still lay there, spread out, and he folded it together and put it in a drawer.

He stripped the brown folders off the papers and put them in a pile. From the pile he selected the New York *Times* and moved to his favorite chair to read.

NEW PEACE CONFERENCE AGREED UPON, said the lead-off headline.

The crisis had been boiling for a month or more, the newest of a long series of crises which had kept the world on edge for years. And the worst of it, Enoch told himself, was that the most of them were manufactured crises, with one side or the other pushing for advantage in the relentless chess game of power politics which had been under way since the end of World War II.

The stories in the *Times* bearing on the conference had a rather desperate, almost fatalistic, ring, as if the writers of the stories, and perhaps the diplomats and all the rest involved, knew the conference would accomplish nothing—if, in fact, it did not serve to make the crisis deeper.

Observers in this capital [wrote one of the *Times's* Washington bureau staff] *are not convinced the conference will serve, in this instance, as similar conferences sometimes have served in the past, to either delay a showdown on the issues or to advance the prospects for a settlement. There is scarcely concealed concern in many quarters that the conference will, instead, fan the flames of controversy higher without, by way of compensation, opening any avenues by which a compromise might seem possible. A conference is popularly supposed to provide a time and place for the sober weighing of the facts and points of argument, but there are few who see in the calling of this conference any indications that this may be the case.*

The coffee maker was going full blast now and Enoch threw the paper down and strode to the stove to snatch it off. From the cupboard he got a cup and went to the table with it.

But before he began to eat, he went back to the desk and, opening a drawer, got out his chart and spread it on the table. Once again he wondered just how valid it might be, although in certain parts of it, at times, it seemed to make a certain sort of sense.

He had based it on the Mizar theory of statistics and had been forced, because of the nature of his subject, to shift some of the factors, to substitute some values. He wondered now, for the thousandth time, if he had made an error somewhere. Had his sifting and substitution destroyed the validity of the system? And if so, how could he correct the errors to restore validity?

Here the factors were, he thought: the birth rate and the total population of the Earth, the death rate, the values of currencies, the spread of living costs, attendance of places of worship, medical advances, technological developments, industrial indices, the labor market, world trade trends—and many others, including some that at first glance might not seem too relevant: the auction price of art objects, vacation preferences and movements, the speed of transportation, the incidence of insanity.

The statistical method developed by the mathematicians of Mizar, he knew, would work anywhere, on anything, if applied correctly. But he had been forced to twist it in translating an alien planet's situation to fit the situation here on Earth—and in consequence of that twisting, did it still apply?

He shuddered as he looked at it. For if he'd made no mistake, if he'd handled everything correctly, if his translations had done no violence to the concept, then the Earth was headed straight for another major war, for a holocaust of nuclear destruction.

He let loose of the corners of the chart and it rolled itself back into a cylinder.

He reached for one of the fruits the Sirrah being had brought him and bit into it. He rolled it on his tongue, savoring the delicacy of the taste. It was, he decided, as good as that strange, birdlike being had guaranteed it would be.

There had been a time, he remembered, when he had held some hope that the chart based on the Mizar theory might show, if not a way to end all war, at least a way to keep the peace. But the chart had never given any hint of the road to peace. Inexorably, relentlessly, it had led the way to war.

How many other wars, he wondered, could the people of the Earth endure?

No man could say, of course, but it might be just one more. For the weapons that would be used in the coming conflict had not as yet been measured and there was no man who could come close to actually estimating the results these weapons would produce.

War had been bad enough when men faced one another with their weapons in their hands, but in any present war great payloads of destruction would go hurtling through the skies to engulf whole cities—aimed not at military concentrations, but at total populations.

He reached out his hand for the chart again, then pulled it back. There was no further need of looking at it. He knew it all by heart. There was no hope in it. He might study it and puzzle over it until the crack of doom and it would not change a whit. There was no hope at all. The world was thundering once again, in a blind red haze of fury and of helplessness, down the road to war.

He went on with his eating and the fruit was even better than it had been at first bite. "Next time," the being had said, "I will bring you more." But it might be a long time before he came again, and he might never come. There were many of them who passed through only once, although there were a few who showed up every week or so—old, regular travelers who had become close friends.

And there had been, he recalled, that little group of Hazers who, years ago, had made arrangements for extra long stopovers at the station so they could sit around this very table and talk the hours away, arriving laden with hampers and with baskets of things to eat and drink, as if it were a picnic.

But finally they had stopped their coming and it had been years since he'd seen any one of them. And he regretted it, for they'd been the best of companions.

He drank an extra cup of coffee, sitting idly in the chair, thinking about those good old days when the band of Hazers came.

His ears caught the faint rustling and he glanced quickly up to see her sitting on the sofa, dressed in the demure hoop skirts of the 1860s.

"Mary!" he said, surprised, rising to his feet.

She was smiling at him in her very special way and she was beautiful, he thought, as no other woman ever had been beautiful.

"Mary," he said, "it's so nice to have you here."

And now, leaning on the mantelpiece, dressed in Union blue, with his belted saber and his full black mustache, was another of his friends.

"Hello, Enoch," David Ransome said. "I hope we don't intrude."

"Never," Enoch told him. "How can two friends intrude?"

He stood beside the table and the past was with him, the good and restful past, the rose-scented and unhaunted past that had never left him.

Somewhere in the distance was the sound of fife and drum and the jangle of the battle harness as the boys marched off to war, with the colonel glorious in his full-dress uniform upon the great black stallion, and the regimental flags snapping in the stiff June breeze.

He walked across the room and over to the sofa. He made a little bow to Mary.

"With your permission, ma'am," he said.

"Please do," she said. "If you should happen to be busy . . ."

"Not at all," he said. "I was hoping you would come."

He sat down on the sofa, not too close to her, and he saw her hands were folded, very primly, in her lap. He wanted to reach out and take her hands in his and hold them for a moment, but he knew he couldn't.

For she wasn't really there.

"It's been almost a week," said Mary, "since I've seen you. How is your work going, Enoch?"

He shook his head. "I still have all the problems. The watchers still are out there. And the chart says war."

David left the mantel and came across the room. He sat down in a chair and arranged his saber.

"War, the way they fight it these days," he declared, "would be a sorry business. Not the way we fought it, Enoch."

"No," said Enoch, "not the way we fought it. And while a war would be bad enough itself, there is something worse. If Earth fights another war, our people will be barred, if not forever, at least for many centuries, from the cofraternity of space."

"Maybe that's not so bad," said David. "We may not be ready to join the ones in space."

"Perhaps not," Enoch admitted. "I rather doubt we are. But we could be some day. And that day would be shoved far into the future if we fight another war. You have to make some pretense of being civilized to join those other races."

"Maybe," Mary said, "they might never know. About a war, I mean. They go no place but this station."

Enoch shook his head. "They would know. I think they're watching us. And anyhow, they would read the papers."

"The papers you subscribe to?"

"I save them for Ulysses. That pile over in the corner. He takes them back to Galactic Central every time he comes. He's very interested in Earth, you know, from the years he spent here. And from Galactic Central, once he'd read them, I have a hunch they travel to the corners of the galaxy."

"Can you imagine," David asked, "what the promotion departments of those newspapers might have to say about it if they only knew their depth of circulation."

Enoch grinned at the thought of it.

"There's that paper down in Georgia," David said, "that covers Dixie like the dew. They'd have to think of something that goes with galaxy."

"Glove," said Mary quickly. "Covers the galaxy like a glove. What do you think of that?"

"Excellent," said David.

"Poor Enoch," Mary said contritely. "Here we make our jokes and Enoch has his problems."

"Not mine to solve, of course," Enoch told her. "I'm just worried by them. All I have to do is stay inside the station and there are no problems. Once you close the door here, the problems of the world are securely locked outside."

"But you can't do that."

"No, I can't," said Enoch.

"I think you may be right," said David, "in thinking that these other races may be watching us. With an eye, perhaps, to some day inviting the human race to join them. Otherwise, why would they have wanted to set up a station here on Earth?"

"They're expanding the network all the time," said Enoch. "They needed a station in this solar system to carry out their extension into this spiral arm."

"Yes, that's true enough," said David, "but it need not have been the Earth. They could have built a station out on Mars and used an alien for a keeper and still have served their purpose."

"I've often thought of that," said Mary. "They wanted a station on the Earth and an Earthman as its keeper. There must be a reason for it."

"I had hoped there was," Enoch told her, "but I'm afraid they came too soon. It's too early for the human race. We aren't grown up. We still are juveniles."

"It's a shame," said Mary. "We'd have so much to learn. They know so much more than we. Their concept of religion, for example."

"I don't know," said Enoch, "whether it's actually a religion. It seems to have few of the trappings we associate with religion. And it is not based on faith. It doesn't have to be. It is based on knowledge. These people know, you see."

"You mean the spiritual force."

"It is there," said Enoch, "just as surely as all the other forces that make up the universe. There is a spiritual force, exactly as there is time and space and gravitation and all the other factors that make up the immaterial universe. It is there and they can establish contact with it . . ."

"But don't you think," asked David, "that the human race may sense this? They don't know it, but they sense it. And are reaching out to touch it. They haven't got the knowledge, so they must do the best they can with faith. And that faith goes back a far way. Back, perhaps, deep into the prehistoric days. A crude faith, then, but a sort of faith, a grasping for a faith."

"I suppose so," Enoch said. "But it actually wasn't the spiritual force I was thinking of. There are all the other things, the material things, the methods, the philosophies that the human race could use. Name almost any branch of science and there is something there for us, more than what we have."

But his mind went back to that strange business of the spiritual force and the even stranger machine which had been built eons ago, by means of which the galactic people were able to establish contact with the force. There was a name for that machine, but there was no word in the English language which closely approximated it. "Talisman" was the closest, but Talisman was too crude a word. Although that had been the word that Ulysses had used when, some years ago, they had talked of it.

There were so many things, so many concepts, he thought, out in the galaxy which could not be adequately expressed in any tongue on Earth. The Talisman was more than a talisman and the machine which had been given the name was more than a mere machine. Involved in it, as well as certain mechanical concepts, was a psychic concept, perhaps some sort of psychic energy that was unknown on Earth. That and a great deal more. He had read some of the literature on the spiritual force and on the Talisman and had realized, he remembered, in the reading of it, how far short he fell, how far short the human race must fall, in an understanding of it.

The Talisman could be operated only by certain beings with certain types of minds and something else besides (could it be, he wondered, with certain kinds of souls?). "Sensitives" was the word he had used in his mental translation of the term for these kinds of people, but once again, he could not be sure if the word came close to fitting. The Talisman was placed in the custody of the most capable, or the most efficient, or the most devoted (whichever it might be) of the galactic sensitives, who carried it from star to star in a sort of eternal progression. And on each planet the people came to make personal and individual contact with the spiritual force through the intervention and the agency of the Talisman and its custodian.

He found that he was shivering at the thought of it—the pure ecstasy of reaching out and touching the spirituality that flooded through the galaxy and, undoubtedly, through the universe. The assurance would be there, he thought, the assurance that life had a special place in the great scheme of existence, that one, no matter how small, how feeble, how insignificant, still did count for something in the vast sweep of space and time.

"What is the trouble, Enoch?" Mary asked.

"Nothing," he said. "I was just thinking. I am sorry. I will pay attention now."

"You were talking," David said, "about what we could find in the galaxy. There was, for one thing, that strange sort of math. You were telling us of it once and it was something . . ."

"The Arcturus math, you mean," said Enoch. "I know little more than when I told you of it. It is too involved. It is based on behavior symbolism."

There was some doubt, he told himself, that you could even call it math, although, by analysis, that was probably what it was. It was something that the scientists of Earth, no doubt, could use to make possible the engineering of the social sciences as logically and as efficiently as the common brand of math had been used to build the gadgets of the Earth.

"And the biology of that race out in Andromeda," Mary said. "The ones who colonized all those crazy planets."

"Yes, I know. But Earth would have to mature a bit in its intellectual and emotional outlook before we'd venture to use it as the Andromedans did. Still, I suppose that it would have its applications."

He shuddered inwardly as he thought of how the Andromedans used it. And that, he knew, was proof that he still was a man of Earth, kin to all the bias and the prejudice and the shibboleths of the human mind. For what the Andromedans had done was only common sense. If you cannot colonize a planet in your present shape, why, then you change your shape. You make yourself into the sort of being that can live upon the planet and then you take it over in that alien shape into which you have changed yourself. If you need to be a worm, then you become a worm—or an insect or a shellfish or whatever it may take. And you change not your body only, but your mind as well, into the kind of mind that will be necessary to live upon that planet.

"There are all the drugs," said Mary, "and the medicines. The medical knowledge that could apply to Earth. There was that little package Galactic Central sent you."

"A packet of drugs," said Enoch, "that could cure almost every ill on Earth. That, perhaps, hurts me most of all. To know they're up there in the cupboard, actually on this planet, where so many people need them."

"You could mail out samples," David said, "to medical associations or to some drug concern."

Enoch shook his head. "I thought of that, of course. But I have the galaxy to consider. I have an obligation to Galactic Central. They have taken great precautions that the station not be known. There are Ulysses and all my other alien friends. I cannot wreck their plans. I cannot play the traitor to them. For when you think of it, Galactic Central and the work it's doing is more important than the Earth."

"Divided loyalties," said David with slight mockery in his tone.

"That is it, exactly. There had been a time, many years ago, when I thought of writing papers for submissions to some of the scientific journals. Not the medical journals, naturally, for I know nothing about medicine. The drugs are there, of course, lying on the shelf, with directions for their use, but they are merely so many pills or powders or ointments, or whatever they may be. But there were other things I knew of, other things I'd learned. Not too much about them, naturally, but at least some hints in some new directions. Enough that someone could pick them up and go on from there. Someone who might know what to do with them."

"But look here," David said, "that wouldn't have worked out. You have no technical nor research background, no educational record. You're not tied up with any school or college. The journals just don't publish you unless you can prove yourself."

"I realize that, of course. That's why I never wrote the papers. I knew there was no use. You can't blame the journals. They must be responsible. Their pages aren't open to just anyone. And even if they had viewed the papers with enough respect to want to publish them, they would have had to find out who I was. And that would have led straight back to the station."

"But even if you could have gotten away with it," David

pointed out, "you'd still not have been clear. You said a while ago you had a loyalty to Galactic Central."

"If," said Enoch, "in this particular case I could have got away with it, it might have been all right. If you just threw out ideas and let some Earth scientists develop them, there'd be no harm done Galactic Central. The main problem, of course, would be not to reveal the source."

"Even so," said David, "there'd be little you actually could tell them. What I mean is that generally you haven't got enough to go on. So much of this galactic knowledge is off the beaten track."

"I know," said Enoch. "The mental engineering of Mankalinen III, for one thing. If the Earth could know of that, our people undoubtedly could find a clue to the treatment of the neurotic and the mentally disturbed. We could empty all the institutions and we could tear them down or use them for something else. There'd be no need of them. But no one other than the people out on Mankalinen III could ever tell us of it. I only know they are noted for their mental engineering, but that is all I know. I haven't the faintest inkling of what it's all about. It's something that you'd have to get from the people out there."

"What you are really talking of," said Mary, "are all the nameless sciences—the ones that no human has ever thought about."

"Like us, perhaps," said David.

"David!" Mary cried.

"There is no sense," said David angrily, "in pretending we are people."

"But you are," said Enoch tensely. "You are people to me. You are the only people that I have. What is the matter, David?"

"I think," said David, "that the time has come to say what we really are. That we are illusion. That we are created and called up. That we exist only for one purpose, to come and talk with you, to fill in for the real people that you cannot have."

"Mary," Enoch cried, "you don't think that way, too! You can't think that way!"

He reached out his arms to her and then he let them drop—terrified at the realization of what he'd been about to do. It was the first time he'd ever tried to touch her. It was the first time, in all the years, that he had forgotten.

"I am sorry, Mary. I should not have done that."

Her eyes were bright with tears.

"I wish you could," she said. "Oh, how I wish you could!"

"David," he said, not turning his head.

"David left," said Mary.

"He won't be back," said Enoch.

Mary shook her head.

"What is the matter, Mary? What is it all about? What have I done!"

"Nothing," Mary said, "except that you made us too much like people. So that we became more human, until we were entirely human. No longer puppets, no longer pretty dolls, but really actual people. I think David must resent it—not that he is people, but that being people, he is still a shadow. It did not matter when we were dolls or puppets, for we were not human then. We had no human feeling."

"Mary, please," he said. "Mary, please forgive me."

She leaned toward him and her face was lighted by deep tenderness. "There is nothing to forgive," she said. "Rather, I suppose, we should thank you for it. You created us out of a love of us and a need of us and it is wonderful to know that you are loved and needed."

"But I don't create you any more," Enoch pleaded. "There was a time, long ago, I had to. But not any longer. Now you come to visit me of your own free will."

How many years? he wondered. It must be all of fifty. And Mary had been the first, and David had been second. Of all the others of them, they had been the first and were the closest and the dearest.

And before that, before he'd even tried, he'd spent other years in studying that nameless science stemming from the thaumaturgists of Alphard XXII.

There had been a day and a state of mind when it would have been black magic, but it was not black magic. Rather, it was the orderly manipulation of certain natural aspects of the universe as yet quite unsuspected by the human race. Perhaps aspects that Man never would discover. For there was not, at least at the present moment, the necessary orientation of the scientific mind to initiate the research that must precede discovery.

"David felt," said Mary, "that we could not go on forever, playing out our little sedate visits. There had to be a time when we faced up to what we really are."

"And the rest of them?"

"I am sorry, Enoch. The rest of them as well."

"But you? How about you, Mary?"

"I don't know," she said. "It is different with me. I love you very much."

"And I . . ."

"No, that's not what I mean. Don't you understand! I'm in love with you."

He sat stricken, staring at her, and there was a great roaring in the world, as if he were standing still and the world and time were rushing swiftly past him.

"If it only could have stayed," she said, "the way it was at first. Then we were glad of our existence and our emotions were so shallow and we seemed to be so happy. Like little happy children, running in the sun. But then we all grew up. And I think I the most of all."

She smiled at him and tears were in her eyes.

"Don't take it so hard, Enoch. We can . . ."

"My dear," he said, "I've been in love with you since the first day that I saw you. I think maybe even before that."

He reached out a hand to her, then pulled it back, remembering.

"I did not know," she said. "I should not have told you. You could live with it until you knew I loved you, too."

He nodded dumbly.

She bowed her head. "Dear God, we don't deserve this. We have done nothing to deserve it."

She raised her head and looked at him. "If I could only touch you."

"We can go on," he said, "as we have always done. You can come to see me any time you want. We can . . ."

She shook her head. "It wouldn't work," she said. "There could neither of us stand it."

He knew that she was right. He knew that it was done. For fifty years she and the others had been dropping in to visit. And they'd come no more. For the fairyland was shattered and the magic spell was broken. He'd be left alone—more alone than ever, more alone than before he'd ever known her.

She would not come again and he could never bring himself to call her up again, even if he could, and his shadow world and his shadow love, the only love he'd ever really had, would be gone forever.

"Good bye, my dear," he said.

But it was too late. She was already gone.

And from far off, it seemed, he heard the moaning whistle that said a message had come in.

13

She had said that they must face up to the kind of things they were.

And what were they? Not, what did he think they were, but what were they, actually? What did they think themselves to be? For perhaps they knew much better than did he.

Where had Mary gone? When she left this room, into what kind of limbo did she disappear? Did she still exist? And if so, what kind of an existence would it be? Would she be stored away somewhere as a little girl would store away her doll in a box pushed back into the closet with all the other dolls?

He tried to imagine limbo and it was a nothingness, and if that were true, a being pushed into limbo would be an existence within a non-existence. There would be nothing—not space nor time, nor light, nor air, no color and no vision, just a never ending nothing that of necessity must lie at some point outside the universe.

Mary! he cried inside himself. *Mary, what have I done to you?*

And the answer lay there, hard and naked.

He had dabbled in a thing which he had not understood. And had, furthermore, committed that greater sin of thinking that he did understand. And the fact of the matter was that he had just barely understood enough to make the concept work, but had not understood enough to be aware of its consequences.

With creation went responsibility and he was not equipped to assume more than the moral responsibility for the wrong that he had done, and moral responsibility, unless it might be coupled with the ability to bring about some mitigation, was an entirely useless thing.

They hated him and resented him and he did not blame them, for he'd led them out and shown them the promised land of humanity and then had led them back. He had given them everything that a human being had with the one exception of that most important thing of all—the ability to exist within the human world.

They all hated him but Mary, and for Mary it was worse than hate. For she was condemned, by the very virtue of the humanity he had given her, to love the monster who had created her.

Hate me, Mary, he pleaded. *Hate me like the others!*

He had thought of them as shadow people, but that had been just a name he'd thought up for himself, for his own convenience, a handy label that he had tagged them with so that he would have some way of identifying them when he thought of them.

But the label had been wrong, for they were not shadowy or ghostlike. To the eyes they were solid and substantial, as real as any people. It was only when you tried to touch them that they were not real—for when you tried to touch them, there was nothing there.

A figment of his mind, he'd thought at first, but now he was not sure. At first they'd come only when he'd called them up, using the knowledge and the techniques that he had acquired in his study of the work done by the thaumaturgists of Alphard XXII. But in recent years he had not called them up. There had been no occasion to. They had anticipated him and come before he could call them up. They sensed his need of them before he knew the need himself. And they were there, waiting for him, to spend an hour or evening.

Figments of his mind in one sense, of course, for he had shaped them, perhaps at the time unconsciously, not knowing why he shaped them so, but in recent years he'd known, although he had tried not to know, would have been the better satisfied if he had not known. For it was a knowledge that he had not admitted, but kept pushed back, far within his mind. But now, when all was gone, when it no longer mattered, he finally did admit it.

David Ransome was himself, as he had dreamed himself to be, as he had wished himself to be—but, of course, as he had never been. He was the dashing Union officer, of not so high a rank as to be stiff and stodgy, but a fair cut above the man of ordinary standing. He was trim and debonair and definitely daredevilish, loved by all the women, admired by all the men. He was a born leader and a good fellow all at once, at home alike in the field or drawing room.

And Mary? Funny, he thought, he had never called her anything but Mary. There had never been a surname. She had been simply Mary.

And she was at least two women, if not more than that. She was Sally Brown, who had lived just down the road—and how long had it been, he wondered, since he'd thought of Sally Brown? It was strange, he knew, that he had not thought of her, that he now was shocked by the memory of a one-time neighbor girl named Sally Brown. For the two of them once had been in love, or only thought, perhaps, that they had been in love. For even in the later years, when he still remembered her, he had never been quite certain, even through the romantic mists of time, if it had been love or no more than the romanticism of a soldier marching off to war. It had been a shy and fumbling, an awkward sort of love, the love of the farmer's daughter for the next-door farmer's son. They had decided to be married when he came home from war, but a few days after Gettysburg he had received the letter, then more than three weeks written, which told him that Sally Brown was dead of diphtheria. He had grieved, he now recalled, but he could not recall how deeply, although it probably had been deeply, for to grieve long and deeply was the fashion in those days.

So Mary very definitely was partly Sally Brown, but not entirely Sally. She was as well that tall, stately daughter of the South, the woman he had seen for a few moments only as he marched a dusty road in the hot Virginia sun. There had been a mansion, one of those great plantation houses, set back from the road, and she had been standing on the portico, beside one of the great white pillars, watching the enemy march past. Her hair was black and her complexion whiter than the pillar and she had stood so straight and proud, so defiant and imperious, that he had remembered her and thought of her and dreamed of her—although he never knew her name—through all the dusty, sweaty, bloody days of war. Wondering as he thought and dreamed of her if the thinking and the dreaming might be unfaithful to his Sally. Sitting around the campfire, when the talk grew quiet, and again, rolled in his blankets, staring at the stars, he had built up a fantasy of how, when the war was ended, he'd go back to that Virginia house and find her. She might be there no longer, but he still would roam the South and find her. But he never did; he had never really meant to find her. It had been a campfire dream.

So Mary had been both of these—she had been Sally Brown and the unknown Virginia belle standing by the pillar to watch the troops march by. She had been the shadow of them and perhaps of many others as yet unrealized by him, a composite of all he had ever known or seen or admired in women. She had been an ideal and perfection. She had been his perfect woman, created in his mind. And now, like Sally Brown, resting in her grave; like the Virginia belle, lost in the mists of time; like all the others who may have contributed to his molding of her, she was gone from him.

And he had loved her, certainly, for she had been a compounding of his loves—a cross section, as it were, of all the women he had ever loved (if he actually had loved any) or the ones he had thought he loved, even in the abstract.

But that she should love him was something that had never crossed his mind. And until he knew her love for him, it had been quite possible to nurse his love of her close inside the heart, knowing that it was a hopeless love and impossible, but the best that he could manage.

He wondered where she might be now, where she had retreated—into the limbo he had attempted to imagine or into some strange non-existence, waiting all unknowing for the time she'd come to him again.

He put up his hands and lowered his head in them and sat in utter misery and guilt, with his face cupped in his fingers.

She would never come again. He prayed she'd never come. It would be better for the both of them if she never came.

If he only could be sure, he thought, of where she might be now. If he only could be certain that she was in a semblance of death and untortured by her thoughts. To believe that she was sentient was more than one could bear.

He heard the hooting of the whistle that said a message waited and he took his head out of his hands. But he did not get up off the sofa.

Numbly his hand reached out to the coffee table that stood before the sofa, its top covered with some of the more colorful of the gewgaws and gimcracks that had been left as gifts by travelers.

He picked up a cube of something that might have been some strange sort of glass or of translucent stone—he had never been able to decide which it was, if either—and cupped it in his hands. Staring into it, he saw a tiny picture, three-dimensional and detailed, of a faery world. It was a prettily grotesque place set inside what might have been a forest glade surrounded by what appeared to be flowering toadstools, and drifting down through the air, as if it might have been a part of the air itself, came what looked for all the world like a shower of jeweled snow, sparkling and glinting in the violet light of a great blue sun. There were things dancing in the glade and they looked more like flowers than animals, but they moved with a grace and poetry that fired one's blood to watch. Then the faery place was wiped out and there was another place—a wild and dismal place, with grim, gaunt, beetling cliffs rearing high against a red and angry sky, while great flying things that looked like flapping dishrags beat their way up and down the cliffs, and there were others of them roosting, most obscenely, upon the scraggly projections that must have been some sort of misshapen trees growing from the very wall of rock. And from far below, from some distance that one could only guess, came the lonesome thundering of a rushing river.

He put the cube back upon the table. He wondered what it was that one saw within its depths. It was like turning the pages of a book, with each page a picture of a different place, but never anything to tell where that place might be. When he first had been given it, he had spent fascinated hours, watching the pictures change as he held it in his hands. There had never been a picture that looked even faintly like any other picture and there was no end to them. One got the feeling that these were not pictures, actually, but that one was looking at the scene itself and that at any moment one might lose his perch upon wherever he was roosting and plunge head first down into the place itself.

But it had finally palled upon him, for it had been a senseless business, gawking at a long series of places that had no identity. Senseless to him, of course, he thought, but not senseless, certainly, to that native of Enif V who had given it to him. It might, for all he knew, Enoch told himself, be of great significance and a treasure of great value.

That was the way it was with so many of the things he had. Even the ones that had given pleasure, he knew, he might be using wrongly, or, at least, in a way that had not been intended.

But there were some—a few, perhaps—that did have a value he could understand and appreciate, although in many instances their functions were of little use to him. There was the tiny clock that gave the local times for all the sectors of the galaxy, and while it might be intriguing, and even essential under certain circumstances, it had little value to him. And there was the perfume mixer, which was as close as he could come in naming it, which allowed a person to create the specific scent desired. Just get the mixture that one wanted and turn it on and the room took on that scent until one should turn it off. He'd had some fun with it, remembering that bitter winter day when, after long experimenting, he had achieved the scent of apple blossoms, and had lived a day in spring while a blizzard howled outside.

He reached out and picked up another piece—a beautiful thing that always had intrigued him, but for which he had never found a use—if, indeed, it had a use. It might be, he told himself, no more than a piece of art, a pretty thing that was meant to look at only. But it had a certain feel (if that were the word) which had led him to believe that it might have some specific function.

It was a pyramid of spheres, succeeding smaller spheres set on larger spheres. Some fourteen inches tall, it was a graceful piece, with each of the spheres a different color—and not just a color painted on, but each color so deep and true that one knew instinctively the color was intrinsic to each sphere, that the entire sphere, from the center of it out to the surface, was all of its particular color.

There was nothing to indicate that any gluelike medium had been used to mount the spheres and hold them in their places. It looked for all the world as if someone had simply piled the spheres, one atop the other, and they had stayed that way.

Holding it in his hands, he tried to recall who had given it to him, but he had no memory of it.

The whistle of the message machine still was calling and there was work to do. He could not sit here, he told himself, mooning the afternoon away. He put the pyramid of spheres back on the table top, and rising, went across the room.

The message said:

NO. 406,302 TO STATION 18327. NATIVE OF VEGA XXI ARRIVING AT 16532.82. DEPARTURE INDETERMINATE. NO LUGGAGE. CABINET ONLY, LOCAL CONDITIONS. CONFIRM.

Enoch felt a glow of happiness, looking at the message. It would be good to have a Hazer once again. It had been a month or more since one had passed through the station.

He could remember back to that first day he had ever met a Hazer, when the five of them had come. It must have been, he thought, back in 1914 or maybe 1915. World War I, which everyone then was calling the Great War, was under way, he knew.

The Hazer would be arriving at about the same time as Ulysses and the three of them could spend a pleasant evening. It was not too often that two good friends ever visited here at once.

He stood a bit aghast at thinking of the Hazer as a friend, for more than likely the being itself was one he had never met. But that made little difference, for a Hazer, any Hazer, would turn out to be a friend.

He got the cabinet in position beneath a materializer unit and double-checked to be sure that everything was exactly as it should be, then went back to the message machine and sent off the confirmation.

And all the time his memory kept on nagging at him. Had it been 1914, or perhaps a little later?

At the catalogue cabinet, he pulled out a drawer and found Vega XXI and the first date listed was July 12, 1915. He found the record book on the shelf and pulled it out and brought it to the desk. He leafed through it rapidly until he found the date.

14

July 12, 1915—Arrived this afternoon (3:20 P.M.) five beings from Vega XXI, the first of their kind to pass through this station. They are biped and humanoid, and one gains the impression that they are not made of flesh—that flesh would be too gross for the kind of things they are—but, of course, they are made of flesh the same as anyone. They glow, not with a visible light, but there is about them an aura that goes with them wherever they may be.

They were, I gathered, a sexual unit, the five of them, although I am not so certain I understand, for it is most confusing. They were happy and friendly and they carried with them an air of faint amusement, not at anything in particular, but at the universe itself, as if they might have enjoyed some sort of cosmic and very private joke that was known to no one else. They were on a holiday and were en route to a festival (although that may not be the precise word for it) on another planet, where other life forms were gathering for a week of carnival. Just how they had been invited or why they had been invited I was unable to determine. It must surely have been a great honor for them to be going there, but so far as I could see they did not seem to think so, but took it as their right. They were very happy and without a care and extremely self-assured and poised, but thinking back on it, I would suppose that they are always that way. I found myself just a little envious at not being able to be as carefree and gay as they were, and trying to imagine how fresh life and the universe must seem to them, and a little resentful that they could be, so unthinkingly, as happy as they were.

I had, according to instructions, hung hammocks so that they could rest, but they did not use them. They brought with them hampers that were filled with food and drink and sat down at my table and began to talk and feast. They asked me to sit with them and they chose two dishes and a bottle, which they assured me would be safe for me to eat and drink, the rest of their fare being somewhat doubtful for a metabolism such as mine. The food was delicious and of a kind I had never tasted—one dish being rather like the rarest and most delicate of old cheeses, and the other of a sweetness that was heavenly. The drink was somewhat like the finest of brandies, yellow in color and no heavier than water.

They asked me about myself and about my planet and they were courteous and seemed genuinely interested and they were quick of understanding in the things I told them. They told me they were headed for a planet the name of which I had not heard before, and they talked among themselves, gaily and happily, but in such a way that I did not seem to be left out. From their talk I gained the fact that some form of art was being presented at the festival on this planet. The art form was not alone of music or painting, but was composed of sound and color and emotion and form and other qualities for which there seem to be no words in the language of the Earth, and which I do not entirely recognize, only gaining the very faintest inkling of what they were talking of in this particular regard. I gained the impression of a three-dimensional symphony, although this is not entirely the right expression, which had been composed, not by a single being, but by a team of beings. They talked of the art form enthusiastically and I seemed to understand that it would last for not only several hours, but for days, and that it was an experience rather than a listening or seeing and that the spectators or audience did not merely sit and listen, but could, if they wished, and must, to get the most out of it, be participants. But I could not understand how they participated and felt I should not ask. They talked of the people they would meet and when they had met them last and gossiped considerably about them, although in kindly fashion, leaving the impression that they and many other people went from planet to planet for some happy purpose. But whether there was any purpose other than enjoyment in their going, I could not determine. I gathered that there might be.

They spoke of other festivals and not all of them were concerned with the one art form, but with other more specialized aspects of the arts, of which I could gain no adequate idea. They seemed to find a great and exuberant happiness in the festivals and it seemed to me that some certain significances aside from the art itself contributed to that happiness. I did not join in this part of their conversation, for, frankly, there was no opportunity. I would have liked to ask some questions, but I had no chance. I suppose that if I had, my questions must have sounded stupid to them, but given the chance, that would not have bothered me too much. And yet in spite of this, they managed somehow to make me feel I was included in their conversation. There was no obvious attempt to do this, and yet they made me feel I was one with them and not simply a station keeper they would spend a short time with. At times they spoke briefly in the language of their planet, which is one of the most beautiful I have ever heard, but for the most part they conversed in the vernacular used by a number of the humanoid races, a sort of pidgin language made up for convenience, and I suspect that this was done out of courtesy to me, and a great courtesy it was. I believe that they were truly the most civilized people I have ever met.

I have said they glowed and I think by that I mean they glowed in spirit. It seemed that they were accompanied, somehow, by a sparkling golden haze that made happy everything it touched—almost as if they moved in some special world that no one else had found. Sitting at the table with them, I seemed to be included in this golden haze and I felt strange, quiet, deep currents of happiness flowing in my veins. I wondered by what route they and their world had arrived at this golden state and if my world could, in some distant time, attain it.

But back of this happiness was a great vitality, the bubbling, effervescent spirit with an inner core of strength and a love of living that seemed to fill every pore of them and every instant of their time.

They had only two hours' time and it passed so swiftly that I had to finally warn them it was time to go. Before they left, they placed two packages on the table and said they were for me and thanked me for my table (what a strange way for them to put it) then they said good bye and stepped into the cabinet (the extra-large one) and I sent them on their way. Even after they were gone, the golden haze seemed to linger in the room and it was hours before all of it was gone. I wished that I might have gone with them to that other planet and its festival.

One of the packages they left contained a dozen bottles of the brandy-like liquor and the bottles themselves were each a piece of art, no two of them alike, being formed of what I am convinced is diamond, but whether fabricated diamond or carved from some great stones, I have no idea. At any rate, I would estimate that each of them is priceless, and each carved in a disturbing variety of symbolisms, each of which, however, has a special beauty of its own. And in the other box was a—well, I suppose that, for lack of other name, you might call it a music box. The box itself is ivory, old yellow ivory that is as smooth as satin, and covered by a mass of diagrammatic carving which must have some significance which I do not understand. On the top of it is a circle set inside a graduated scale and when I turned the circle to the first graduation there was music and through all the room an interplay of many-colored light, as if the entire room was filled with different kinds of color, and through it all a far-off suggestion of that golden haze. And from the box came, too, perfumes that filled the room, and feeling, emotion—whatever one may call it—but something that took hold of one and made one sad or happy or whatever might go with the music and the color and perfume. Out of that box came a world in which one lived out the composition or whatever it might be—living it with all that one had in him, all the emotion and belief and intellect of which one is capable. And here, I am quite certain, was a recording of that art form of which they had been talking. And not one composition alone, but 206 of them, for that is the number of the graduation marks and for each mark there is a separate composition. In the days to come I shall play them all and make notes upon each of them and assign them names, perhaps, according to their characteristics, and from them, perhaps, can gain some knowledge as well as entertainment.

15

The twelve diamond bottles, empty long ago, stood in a sparkling row upon the fireplace mantel. The music box, as

one of his choicest possessions, was stored inside one of the cabinets, where no harm could come to it. And Enoch thought rather
ruefully, in all these years, despite regular use of it, he had not
as yet played through the entire list of compositions. There were
so many of the early ones that begged for a replaying that he
was not a great deal more than halfway through the graduated
markings.

The Hazers had come back, the five of them, time and time
again, for it seemed that they found in this station, perhaps
even in the man who operated it, some quality that pleased
them. They had helped him learn the Vegan language and had
brought him scrolls of Vegan literature and many other things,
and had been, without any doubt, the best friends among the
aliens (other than Ulysses) that he had ever had. Then one day
they came no more and he wondered why, asking after them
when other Hazers showed up at the station. But he had never
learned what had happened to them.

He knew far more now about the Hazers and their art forms,
their traditions and their customs and their history, than he'd
known that first day he'd written of them, back in 1915. But he
still was far from grasping many of the concepts that were com-
monplace with them.

There had been many of them since that day in 1915 and
there was one he remembered in particular—the old, wise one,
the philosopher, who had died on the floor beside the sofa.

They had been sitting on the sofa, talking, and he even could
remember the subject of their talk. The old one had been telling
of the perverse code of ethics, at once irrational and comic, which
had been built up by that curious race of social vegetables he
had encountered on one of his visits to an off-track planet on
the other side of the galactic rim. The old Hazer had a drink or
two beneath his belt and he was in splendid form, relating incident after incident with enthusiastic gusto.

Suddenly, in mid-sentence, he had stopped his talking, and
had slumped quietly forward. Enoch, startled, reached for him,

but before he could lay a hand upon him, the old alien had slid slowly to the floor.

The golden haze had faded from his body and slowly flickered out and the body lay there, angular and bony and obscene, a terribly alien thing there upon the floor, a thing that was at once pitiful and monstrous. More monstrous, it seemed to Enoch, than anything in alien form he had ever seen before.

In life it had been a wondrous creature, but now, in death, it was an old bag of hideous bones with a scaly parchment stretched to hold the bones together. It was the golden haze, Enoch told himself, gulping, in something near to horror, that had made the Hazer seem so wondrous and so beautiful, so vital, so alive and quick, so filled with dignity. The golden haze was the life of them and when the haze was gone, they became mere repulsive horrors that one gagged to look upon.

Could it be, he wondered, that the goldenness was the Hazers' life force and that they wore it like a cloak, as a sort of over-all disguise? Did they wear their life force on the outside of them while all other creatures wore it on the inside?

A piteous little wind was lamenting in the gingerbread high up in the gables and through the windows he could see battalions of tattered clouds fleeing in ragged retreat across the moon, which had climbed halfway up the eastern sky.

There was a coldness and a loneliness in the station—a far-reaching loneliness that stretched out and out, farther than mere Earth loneliness could go.

Enoch turned from the body and walked stiffly across the room to the message machine. He put in a call for a connection direct with Galactic Central, then stood waiting, gripping the sides of the machine with both his hands.

GO AHEAD, said Galactic Central.

Briefly, as objectively as he was able, Enoch reported what had happened.

There was no hesitation and there were no questions from the other end. Just the simple directions (as if this was something that happened all the time) of how the situation should be handled. The Vegan must remain upon the planet of its death, its body to be disposed of according to the local customs obtaining on that planet. For that was the Vegan law, and, likewise, a point of honor. A Vegan, when he fell, must stay where he fell, and that place became, forever, a part of Vega XXI. There were such places, said Galactic Central, all through the galaxy.

THE CUSTOM HERE [typed Enoch] IS TO INTER THE DEAD.

THEN INTER THE VEGAN.

WE READ A VERSE OR TWO FROM OUR HOLY BOOK.

READ ONE FOR THE VEGAN, THEN. YOU CAN DO ALL THIS?

YES. BUT WE USUALLY HAVE IT DONE BY A PRACTITIONER OF RELIGION. UNDER THE PRESENT CIRCUMSTANCES, HOWEVER, THAT MIGHT BE UNWISE.

AGREED [said Galactic Central] YOU CAN DO AS WELL YOURSELF?

I CAN.

IT IS BEST, THEN, THAT YOU DO.

WILL THERE BE RELATIVES OR FRIENDS ARRIVING FOR THE RITES?

NO.

YOU WILL NOTIFY THEM?

FORMALLY, OF COURSE. BUT THEY ALREADY KNOW.

HE ONLY DIED A MOMENT OR TWO AGO.

NEVERTHELESS, THEY KNOW.

WHAT ABOUT A DEATH CERTIFICATE?

NONE IS NEEDED. THEY KNOW OF WHAT HE DIED.

HIS LUGGAGE? THERE IS A TRUNK.

KEEP IT. IT IS YOURS. IT IS A TOKEN FOR THE
SERVICES YOU PERFORM FOR THE HONORED
DEAD. THAT ALSO IS THE LAW.

BUT THERE MAY BE IMPORTANT MATTERS IN
IT.

YOU WILL KEEP THE TRUNK. TO REFUSE
WOULD INSULT THE MEMORY OF THE DEAD.
ANYTHING ELSE? [asked Enoch] THAT IS ALL?
THAT IS ALL. PROCEED AS IF THE VEGAN
WERE ONE OF YOUR OWN.

Enoch cleared the machine and went back across the room.
He stood above the Hazer, getting up his nerve to bend and
lift the body to place it on the sofa. He shrank from touching
it. It was so unclean and terrible, such a travesty on the shining
creature that had sat there talking with him.

Since he met the Hazers he had loved them and admired
them, had looked forward to each visit by them—by any one
of them. And now he stood, a shivering coward who could not
touch one dead.

It was not the horror only, for in his years as keeper of the
station, he had seen much of pure visual horror as portrayed in
alien bodies. And yet he had learned to submerge that sense of
horror, to disregard the outward appearance of it, to regard all
life as brother life, to meet all things as people.

It was something else, he knew, some other unknown factor
quite apart from horror, that he felt. And yet this thing, he reminded himself, was a friend of his. And as a dead friend, it
demanded honor from him, it demanded love and care.

Blindly he drove himself to the task. He stooped and lifted
it. It had almost no weight at all, as if in death it had lost a
dimension of itself, had somehow become a smaller thing and
less significant. Could it be, he wondered, that the golden haze
might have a weight all of its own?

He laid the body on the sofa and straightened it as best he

could. Then he went outside and, lighting the lantern in the shed, went down to the barn.

It had been years since he had been there, but nothing much had changed. Protected by a tight roof from the weather, it had stayed snug and dry. There were cobwebs hanging from the beams and dust was everywhere. Straggling clumps of ancient hay, stored in the mow above, hung down through the cracks in the boards that floored the mow. The place had a dry, sweet, dusty smell about it, all the odors of animals and manure long gone.

Enoch hung the lantern on the peg behind the row of stanchions and climbed the ladder to the mow. Working in the dark, for he dared not bring the lantern into this dust heap of dried-out hay, he found the pile of oaken boards far beneath the eaves.

Here, he remembered, underneath these slanting eaves, had been a pretended cave in which, as a boy, he had spent many happy rainy days when he could not be outdoors. He had been Robinson Crusoe in his desert island cave, or some now nameless outlaw hiding from a posse, or a man holed up against the threat of scalp-hunting Indians. He had had a gun, a wooden gun that he had sawed out of a board, working it down later with draw-shave and knife and a piece of glass to scrape it smooth. It had been something he had cherished through all his boyhood days—until that day, when he had been twelve, that his father, returning home from a trip to town, had handed him a rifle for his very own.

He explored the stack of boards in the dark, determining by feel the ones that he would need. These he carried to the ladder and carefully slid down to the floor below.

Climbing down the ladder, he went up the short flight of stairs to the granary, where the tools were stored. He opened the lid of the great tool chest and found that it was filled with long deserted mice nests. Pulling out handfuls of the straw and hay and grass that the rodents had used to set up their one-time housekeeping, he uncovered the tools. The shine had gone from them, their surface grayed by the soft patina that came from long disuse, but there was no rust upon them and the cutting edges still retained their sharpness.

Selecting the tools he needed, he went back to the lower part of the barn and fell to work. A century ago, he thought, he had done as he was doing now, working by lantern light to construct a coffin. And that time it had been his father lying in the house.

The oaken boards were dry and hard, but the tools still were in shape to handle them. He sawed and planed and hammered and there was the smell of sawdust. The barn was snug and silent, the depth of hay standing in the mow drowning out the noise of the complaining wind outside.

He finished the coffin and it was heavier than he had figured, so he found the old wheelbarrow, leaning against the wall back of the stalls that once had been used for horses, and loaded the coffin on it. Laboriously, stopping often to rest, he wheeled it down to the little cemetery inside the apple orchard.

And here, beside his father's grave, he dug another grave, having brought a shovel and a pickax with him. He did not dig it as deep as he would have liked to dig, not the full six feet that was decreed by custom, for he knew that if he dug it that deep he never would be able to get the coffin in. So he dug it slightly less than four, laboring in the light of the lantern, set atop the mound of dirt to cast its feeble glow. An owl came up from the woods and sat for a while, unseen, somewhere in the orchard, muttering and gurgling in between its hoots. The moon sank toward the west and the ragged clouds thinned out to let the stars shine through.

Finally it was finished, with the grave completed and the casket in the grave and the lantern flickering, the kerosene almost gone, and the chimney blacked from the angle at which the lantern had been canted.

Back at the station, Enoch hunted up a sheet in which to wrap the body. He put a Bible in his pocket and picked up the shrouded Vegan and, in the first faint light that preceded dawn, marched down to the apple orchard. He put the Vegan in the coffin and nailed shut the lid, then climbed from the grave.

Standing on the edge of it, he took the Bible from his pocket and found the place he wanted. He read aloud, scarcely needing to strain his eyes in the dim light to follow the text, for it was from a chapter that he had read many times:

In my Father's house are many mansions; if it were not so, I would have told you . . .

Thinking, as he read it, how appropriate it was; how there must need be many mansions in which to house all the souls in the galaxy—and of all the other galaxies that stretched, perhaps interminably, through space. Although if there were understanding, one might be enough.

He finished reading and recited the burial service, from memory, as best he could, not being absolutely sure of all the words. But sure enough, he told himself, to make sense out of it. Then he shoveled in the dirt.

The stars and moon were gone and the wind had died. In the quietness of the morning, the eastern sky was pearly pink.

Enoch stood beside the grave, with the shovel in his hand. "Good bye, my friend," he said.

Then he turned and, in the first flush of the morning, went back to the station.

16

Enoch got up from his desk and carried the record book back to the shelf and slid it into place.

He turned around and stood hesitantly.

There were things that he should do. He should read his papers. He should be writing up his journal. There were a couple of papers in the latest issues of the *Journal of Geophysical Research* that he should be looking at.

But he didn't feel like doing any of them. There was too much to think about, too much to worry over, too much to mourn.

The watchers still were out there. He had lost his shadow people. And the world was edging in toward war.

Although, perhaps, he should not be worrying about what happened to the world. He could renounce the world, could resign from the human race any time he wished. If he never went outside, if he never opened up the door, then it would make no difference to him what the world might do or what might happen to it. For he had a world. He had a greater world than anyone outside this station had ever dreamed about. He did not need the Earth.

But even as he thought it, he knew he could not make it stick. For, in a very strange and funny way, he still did need the Earth.

He walked over to the door and spoke the phrase and the door came open. He walked into the shed and it closed behind him.

He went around the corner of the house and sat down on the steps that led up to the porch.

This, he thought, was where it all had started. He had been sitting here that summer day of long ago when the stars had reached out across vast gulfs of space and put the finger on him.

The sun was far down the sky toward the west and soon it would be evening. Already the heat of the day was falling off, with a faint, cool breeze creeping up out of the hollow that ran down to the river valley. Down across the field, at the edge of the woods, crows were wheeling in the sky and cawing.

It would be hard to shut the door, he knew, and keep it shut. Hard never to feel the sun or wind again, to never know the smell of the changing seasons as they came across the Earth. Man, he told himself, was not ready for that. He had not as yet become so totally a creature of his own created environment that he could divorce entirely the physical characteristics of his native planet. He needed sun and soil and wind to remain a man.

He should do this oftener, Enoch thought, come out here and sit, doing nothing, just looking, seeing the trees and the river to the west and the blue of the Iowa hills across the Mississippi, watching the crows wheeling in the skies and the pigeons strutting on the ridgepole of the barn.

It would be worth while each day to do it, for what was another hour of aging? He did not need to save his hours—not now he didn't. There might come a time when he'd become very jealous of them and when that day came, he could hoard the hours and minutes, even the seconds, in as miserly a fashion as he could manage.

He heard the sound of the running feet as they came around the farther corner of the house, a stumbling, exhausted running, as if the one who ran might have come a far way.

He leapt to his feet and strode out into the yard to see who it might be and the runner came stumbling toward him, with her arms outstretched. He put out an arm and caught her as she came close to him, holding her close against him so she would not fall.

"Lucy!" he cried. "Lucy! What has happened, child?"

His hands against her back were warm and sticky and he took one of them away to see that it was smeared with blood. The back of her dress, he saw, was soaked and dark.

He grabbed her by the shoulders and shoved her away from him so he could see her face. It was wet with crying and there was terror in the face—and pleading with the terror.

She pulled away from him and turned around. Her hands came up and slipped her dress off her shoulders and let it slide halfway down her back. The flesh of the shoulders were ribboned by long slashes that still were oozing blood.

She pulled the dress up again and turned to face him. She

made a pleading gesture and pointed backward down the hill, in the direction of the field that ran down to the woods.

There was motion down there, someone coming through the woods, almost at the edge of the old deserted field.

She must have seen it, too, for she came close against him, shivering, seeking his protection.

He bent and lifted her in his arms and ran for the shed. He spoke the phrase and the door came open and he stepped into the station. Behind him he heard the door go sliding shut.

Once inside, he stood there, with Lucy Fisher cradled in his arms, and knew that what he'd done had been a great mistake— that it was something that, in a sober moment, he never would have done, that if he'd given it a second thought, he would not have done it.

But he had acted on an impulse, with no thought at all. The girl had asked protection and here she had protection, here nothing in the world ever could get at her. But she was a human being and no human being, other than himself, should have ever crossed the threshold.

But it was done and there was no way to change it. Once across the threshold, there was no way to change it.

He carried her across the room and put her on the sofa, then stepped back. She sat there, looking up at him, smiling very faintly, as if she did not know if she were allowed to smile in a place like this. She lifted a hand and tried to brush away the tears that were upon her cheeks.

She looked quickly around the room and her mouth made an O of wonder.

He squatted down and patted the sofa and shook a finger at her, hoping that she might understand that he meant she should stay there, that she must go nowhere else. He swept an arm in a motion to take in all the remainder of the station and shook his head as sternly as he could.

She watched him, fascinated, then she smiled and nodded, as if she might have understood.

He reached out and took one of her hands in his own, and holding it, patted it as gently as he could, trying to reassure her, to make her understand that everything was all right if she only stayed exactly where she was.

She was smiling now, not wondering, apparently, if there were any reason that she should not smile.

She reached out her free hand and made a little fluttering gesture toward the coffee table, with its load of alien gadgets.

He nodded and she picked up one of them, turning it admiringly in her hand.

He got to his feet and went to the wall to take down the rifle.

Then he went outside to face whatever had been pursuing her.

17

Two men were coming up the field toward the house and Enoch saw that one of them was Hank Fisher, Lucy's father. He had met the man, rather briefly, several years ago, on one of his walks. Hank had explained, rather sheepishly and when no explanation had been necessary, that he was hunting for a cow which had strayed away. But from his furtive manner, Enoch had deduced that his errand, rather than the hunting of a cow, had been somewhat on the shady side, although he could not imagine what it might have been.

The other man was younger. No more, perhaps, than sixteen or seventeen. More than likely, Enoch told himself, he was one of Lucy's brothers.

Enoch stood by the porch and waited.

Hank, he saw, was carrying a coiled whip in his hand, and looking at it, Enoch understood those wounds on Lucy's shoulders. He felt a swift flash of anger, but tried to fight it down. He could deal better with Hank Fisher if he kept his temper.

The two men stopped three paces or so away.

"Good afternoon," said Enoch.

"You seen my gal?" asked Hank.

"And if I have?" asked Enoch.

"I'll take the hide off of her," yelled Hank, flourishing the whip.

"In such a case," said Enoch, "I don't believe I'll tell you anything."

"You got her hid," charged Hank.

"You can look around," said Enoch.

Hank took a quick step forward, then thought better of it.

"She got what she had coming to her," he yelled. "And I ain't finished with her yet. There ain't no one, not even my own flesh and blood, can put a hex on me."

Enoch said nothing. Hank stood, undecided.

"She meddled," he said. "She had no call to meddle. It was none of her damn' business."

The young man said, "I was just trying to train Butcher. Butcher," he explained to Enoch, "is a coon hound pup."

"That is right," said Hank. "He wasn't doing nothing wrong. The boys caught a young coon the other night. Took a lot of doing. Roy, here, had staked out the coon—tied it to a tree. And he had Butcher on a leash. He was letting Butcher fight the coon. Not hurting anything. He'd pull Butcher off before any damage could be done and let them rest a while. Then he'd let Butcher at the coon again."

"It's the best way in the world," said Roy, "to get a coon dog trained."

"That is right," said Hank. "That is why they caught the coon."

"We needed it," said Roy, "to train this Butcher pup."

"This all is fine," said Enoch, "and I am glad to hear it. But what has it got to do with Lucy?"

"She interfered," said Hank. "She tried to stop the training. She tried to grab Butcher away from Roy, here."

"For a dummy," Roy said, "she is a mite too uppity."

"You hush your mouth," his father told him sternly, swinging around on him.

Roy mumbled to himself, falling back a step.

Hank turned back to Enoch.

"Roy knocked her down," he said. "He shouldn't have done that. He should have been more careful."

"I didn't mean to," Roy said. "I just swung my arm out to keep her away from Butcher."

"That is right," said Hank. "He swung a bit too hard. But there wasn't any call for her doing what she did. She tied Butcher up in knots so he couldn't fight that coon. Without laying a finger on him, mind you, she tied him up in knots. He couldn't move a muscle. That made Roy mad."

He appealed to Enoch, earnestly, "Wouldn't that have made you mad?"

"I don't think it would," said Enoch. "But then, I'm not a coon-dog man."

Hank stared in wonder at this lack of understanding.

But he went on with his story. "Roy got real mad at her. He'd raised that Butcher. He thought a lot of him. He wasn't going to let no one, not even his own sister, tie that dog in knots. So he went after her and she tied him up in knots, just like she did to Butcher. I never seen a thing like it in all my born days. Roy just stiffened up and then he fell down to the ground and his legs pulled up against his belly and he wrapped his arms around himself and he laid there on the ground, pulled into a ball. Him and Butcher, both. But she never touched that coon. She never tied him in no knots. Her own folks is all she touched."

"It didn't hurt," said Roy. "It didn't hurt at all."

"I was sitting there," said Hank, "braiding this here bull whip. Its end had frayed and I fixed a new one on it. And I seen it all, but I didn't do a thing until I saw Roy there, tied up on the ground. And I figured then it had gone far enough. I am a broad-minded man; I don't mind a little wart-charming and other piddling things like that. There have been a lot of people who have been able to do that. It ain't no disgrace at all. But this thing of tying dogs and people into knots . . ."

"So you hit her with the whip," said Enoch.

"I did my duty," Hank told him solemnly. "I ain't about to have no witch in any family of mine. I hit her a couple of licks and her making that dumb show of hers to try to get me stopped. But I had my duty and I kept on hitting. If I did enough of it, I figured, I'd knock it out of her. That was when she put the hex on me. Just like she did on Roy and Butcher, but in a different way. She turned me blind—she blinded her own father! I couldn't see a thing. I just stumbled around the yard, yelling and clawing at my eyes. And then they got all right again, but she was gone. I saw her running through the woods and up the hill. So Roy and me, we took out after her."

"And you think I have her here?"

"I know you have," said Hank.

"O.K.," said Enoch. "Have a look around."

"You can bet I will," Hank told him grimly. "Roy, take the barn. She might be hiding there."

Roy headed for the barn. Hank went into the shed, came out almost immediately, strode down to the sagging chicken house.

Enoch stood and waited, the rifle cradled on his arm.

He had trouble here, he knew—more trouble than he'd ever had before. There was no such thing as reasoning with a man of Hank Fisher's stripe. There was no approach, right now, that he would understand. All that he could do, he knew, was to wait until Hank's temper had cooled off. Then there might be an outside chance of talking sense to him.

The two of them came back.

"She ain't nowhere around," said Hank. "She is in the house."

Enoch shook his head. "There can't anyone get into that house."

"Roy," said Hank, "climb them there steps and open up that door."

Roy looked fearfully at Enoch.

"Go ahead," said Enoch.

Roy moved forward slowly and went up the steps. He crossed the porch and put his hand upon the front door knob and turned. He tried again. He turned around.

"Pa," he said, "I can't turn it. I can't get it open."

"Hell," said Hank, disgusted, "you can't do anything."

Hank took the steps in two jumps, paced wrathfully across the porch. His hand reached out and grasped the knob and wrenched at it powerfully. He tried again and yet again. He turned angrily to face Enoch.

"What is going on here?" he yelled.

"I told you," Enoch said, "that you can't get in."

"The hell I can't!" roared Hank.

He tossed the whip to Roy and came down off the porch, striding over to the woodpile that stood beside the shed. He wrenched the heavy, double-bitted ax out of the chopping block.

"Careful with that ax," warned Enoch. "I've had it for a long time and I set a store by it."

Hank did not answer. He went up on the porch and squared off before the door.

"Stand off," he said to Roy. "Give me elbow room."

Roy backed away.

"Wait a minute," Enoch said. "You mean to chop down that door?"

"You're damned right I do."

Enoch nodded gravely.

"Well?" asked Hank.

"It's all right with me if you want to try."

Hank took his stance, gripping the handle of the ax. The steel flashed swiftly, up over his shoulder, then down in a driven blow.

The edge of the steel struck the surface of the door and turned, deflected by the surface, changed its course, bouncing from the door. The blade came slicing down and back. It missed Hank's spraddled leg by no more than an inch and the momentum of it spun him half around.

He stood there, foolishly, arms outstretched, hands still gripping the handle of the ax. He stared at Enoch.

"Try again," invited Enoch.

Rage flowed over Hank. His face was flushed with anger. "By God, I will!" he yelled.

He squared off again and this time he swung the ax, not at the door, but at the window set beside the door.

The blade struck and there was a high singing sound as pieces of sun-bright steel went flying through the air.

Ducking away, Hank dropped the ax. It fell to the floor of the porch and bounced. One blade was broken, the metal sheared away in jagged breaks. The window was intact. There was not a scratch upon it.

Hank stood there for a moment, staring at the broken ax, as if he could not quite believe it.

Silently he stretched out his hand and Roy put the bull whip in it.

The two of them came down the stairs.

They stopped at the bottom of them and looked at Enoch. Hank's hand twitched on the whip.

"If I were you," said Enoch, "I wouldn't try it, Hank. I can move awfully fast."

He patted the gun butt. "I'd have the hand off you before you could swing that whip."

Hank breathed heavily. "There's the devil in you, Wallace," he said. "And there's the devil in her, too. You're working together, the two of you. Sneaking around in the woods, meeting one another."

Enoch waited, watching the both of them.

"God help me," cried Hank. "My own daughter is a witch!"

"I think," said Enoch, "you should go back home. If I happen to find Lucy, I will bring her there."

Neither of them made a move.

"You haven't heard the last of this," yelled Hank. "You have my daughter somewhere and I'll get you for it."

"Any time you want," said Enoch, "but not now."

He made an imperative gesture with the rifle barrel.

"Get moving," he said. "And don't come back. Either one of you."

They hesitated for a moment, looking at him, trying to gauge him, trying to guess what he might do next.

Slowly they turned and, walking side by side, moved off down the hill.

18

He should have killed the two of them, he thought. They were not fit to live.

He glanced down at the rifle and saw that his hands had such a tense grip on the gun that his fingers stood out white and stiff against the satin brownness of the wood.

He gasped a little in his effort to fight down the rage that boiled inside him, trying to explode. If they had stayed here any longer, if he'd not run them off, he knew he'd have given in to that towering rage.

And it was better, much better, the way that it had been. He wondered a little dully how he had managed to hold in.

And was glad he had. For even as it stood, it would be bad enough.

They would say he was a madman; that he had run them off

at gunpoint. They might even say that he had kidnaped Lucy and was holding her against her will. They would stop at nothing to make him all the trouble that they could.

He had no illusions about what they might do, for he knew the breed, vindictive in their smallness—little vicious insects of the human race.

He stood beside the porch and watched them down the hill, wondering how a girl so fine as Lucy could spring from such decadent stock. Perhaps her handicap had served as a bulwark against the kind of folks they were; had kept her from becoming another one of them. Perhaps if she could have talked with them or listened, she would in time have become as shiftless and as vicious as any one of them.

It had been a great mistake to get mixed up in a thing like this. A man in his position had no business in an involvement such as this. He had too much to lose; he should have stood aside.

And yet what could he have done? Could he have refused to give Lucy his protection, with the blood soaking through her dress from the lashes that lay across her shoulders? Should he have ignored the frantic, helpless pleading in her face?

He might have done it differently, he thought. There might have been other, smarter ways in which to handle it. But there had been no time to think of any smarter way. There only had been time to carry her to safety and then go outside to meet them.

And now, that he thought of it, perhaps the best thing would have been not to go outside at all. If he'd stayed inside the station, nothing would have happened.

It had been impulsive, that going out to face them. It had been, perhaps, the human thing to do, but it had not been wise. But he had done it and it was over now and there was no turning back. If he had it to do again, he would do it differently, but you got no second chance.

He turned heavily around and went back inside the station.

Lucy was still sitting on the sofa and she held a flashing object in her hand. She was staring at it raptly and there was in her face again that same vibrant and alert expression he had seen that morning when she'd held the butterfly.

He laid the rifle on the desk and stood quietly there, but she must have caught the motion of him, for she looked quickly up. And then her eyes once more went back to the flashing thing she was holding in her hands.

He saw that it was the pyramid of spheres and now all the spheres were spinning slowly, in alternating clockwise and counterclockwise motions, and that as they spun they shone and glittered, each in its own particular color, as if there might be, deep inside each one of them, a source of soft, warm light.

Enoch caught his breath at the beauty and the wonder of it— the old, hard wonder of what this thing might be and what it might be meant to do. He had examined it a hundred times or more and had puzzled at it and there had been nothing he could find that was of significance. So far as he could see, it was only something that was meant to be looked at, although there had been that persistent feeling that it had a purpose and that, perhaps, somehow, it was meant to operate.

And now it was in operation. He had tried a hundred times to get it figured out and Lucy had picked it up just once and had got it figured out.

He noticed the rapture with which she was regarding it. Was it possible, he wondered, that she knew its purpose?

He went across the room and touched her arm and she lifted her face to look at him and in her eyes he saw the gleam of happiness and excitement.

He made a questioning gesture toward the pyramid, trying to ask if she knew what it might be. But she did not understand him. Or perhaps she knew, but knew as well how impossible it would be to explain its purpose. She made that happy, fluttery motion with her hand again, indicating the table with its load of gadgets and she seemed to try to laugh—there was, at least, a sense of laughter in her face.

Just a kid, Enoch told himself, with a box heaped high with new and wondrous toys. Was that all it was to her? Was she happy and excited merely because she suddenly had become aware of all the beauty and the novelty of the things stacked there on the table?

He turned wearily and went back to the desk. He picked up the rifle and hung it on the pegs.

She should not be in the station. No human being other than himself should ever be inside the station. Bringing her here, he had broken that unspoken understanding he had with the aliens who had installed him as a keeper. Although, of all the humans he could have brought, Lucy was the one who could possibly be exempt from the understood restriction. For she could never tell the things that she had seen.

She could not remain, he knew. She must be taken home. For if she were not taken, there would be a massive hunt for her, a lost girl—a beautiful deaf-mute.

A story of a missing deaf-mute girl would bring in newspapermen in a day or two. It would be in all the papers and on television and on radio and the woods would be swarming with hundreds of searchers.

Hank Fisher would tell how he'd tried to break into the house and couldn't and there'd be others who would try to break into the house and there'd be hell to pay.

Enoch sweated, thinking of it.

All the years of keeping out of people's way, all the years of being unobtrusive would be for nothing then. This strange house upon a lonely ridge would become a mystery for the world, and a challenge and a target for all the crackpots of the world.

He went to the medicine cabinet, to get the healing ointment that had been included in the drug packet provided by Galactic Central.

He found it and opened the little box. More than half of it

remained. He'd used it through the years, but sparingly. There was, in fact, little need to use a great deal of it.

He went across the room to where Lucy sat and stood back of the sofa. He showed her what he had and made motions to show her what it was for. She slid her dress off her shoulders and he bent to look at the slashes.

The bleeding had stopped, but the flesh was red and angry. Gently he rubbed ointment into the stripes that the whip had made.

She had healed the butterfly, he thought; but she could not heal herself.

On the table in front of her the pyramid of spheres still was flashing and glinting, throwing a flickering shadow of color all about the room.

It was operating, but what could it be doing?

It was finally operating, but not a thing was happening as a result of that operation.

19

Ulysses came as twilight was deepening into night. Enoch and Lucy had just finished with their supper and were sitting at the table when Enoch heard his footsteps.

The alien stood in shadow and he looked, Enoch thought, more than ever like the cruel clown. His lithe, flowing body had the look of smoked, tanned buckskin. The patchwork color of his hide seemed to shine with a faint luminescence and the sharp, hard angles of his face, the smooth baldness of his head, the flat, pointed ears pasted tight against the skull lent him a vicious fearsomeness.

If one did not know him for the gentle character that he was,

Enoch told himself, he would be enough to scare a man out of
seven years of growth.

"We had been expecting you," said Enoch. "The coffeepot is
boiling."

Ulysses took a slow step forward, then paused.

"You have another with you. A human, I would say."

"There is no danger," Enoch told him.

"Of another gender. A female, is it not? You have found a
mate?"

"No," said Enoch. "She is not my mate."

"You have acted wisely through the years," Ulysses told him.
"In a position such as yours, a mate is not the best."

"You need not worry. There is a malady upon her. She has
no communication. She can neither hear nor speak."

"A malady?"

"Yes, from the moment she was born. She has never heard
or spoken. She can tell of nothing here."

"Sign language?"

"She knows no sign language. She refused to learn it."

"She is a friend of yours."

"For some years," said Enoch. "She came seeking my protection. Her father used a whip to beat her."

"This father knows she's here?"

"He thinks she is, but he cannot know."

Ulysses came slowly out of the darkness and stood within
the light.

Lucy was watching him, but there was no terror on her face.
Her eyes were level and untroubled and she did not flinch.

"She takes me well," Ulysses said. "She does not run or
scream."

"She could not scream," said Enoch, "even if she wished."

"I must be most repugnant," Ulysses said, "at first sight to
any human."

"She does not see the outside only. She sees inside of you as
well."

"Would she be frightened if I made a human bow to her?"

"I think," said Enoch, "she might be very pleased."

Ulysses made his bow, formal and exaggerated, with one hand upon his leathery belly, bowing from the waist.

Lucy smiled and clapped her hands.

"You see," Ulysses cried, delighted, "I think that she may like me."

"Why don't you sit down, then," suggested Enoch, "and we all will have some coffee."

"I had forgotten of the coffee. The sight of this other human drove coffee from my mind."

He sat down at the place where the third cup had been set and waiting for him. Enoch started around the table, but Lucy rose and went to get the coffee.

"She understands?" Ulysses asked.

Enoch shook his head. "You sat down by the cup and the cup was empty."

She poured the coffee, then went over to the sofa.

"She will not stay with us?" Ulysses asked.

"She's intrigued by that tableful of trinkets. She set one of them to going."

"You plan to keep her here?"

"I can't keep her," Enoch said. "There'll be a hunt for her. I'll have to take her home."

"I do not like it," Ulysses said.

"Nor do I. Let's admit at once that I should not have brought her here. But at the time it seemed the only thing to do. I had no time to think it out."

"You've done no wrong," said Ulysses softly.

"She cannot harm us," said Enoch. "Without communication . . ."

"It's not that," Ulysses told him. "She's just a complication and I do not like further complications. I came tonight to tell you, Enoch, that we are in trouble."

"Trouble? But there's not been any trouble."

Ulysses lifted his coffee cup and took a long drink of it.

"That is good," he said. "I carry back the bean and make it at my home. But it does not taste the same."

"This trouble?"

"You remember the Vegan that died here several of your years ago."

Enoch nodded. "The Hazer."

"The being has a proper name . . ."

Enoch laughed. "You don't like our nicknames."

"It is not our way," Ulysses said.

"My name for them," said Enoch, "is a mark of my affection."

"You buried this Vegan."

"In my family plot," said Enoch. "As if he were my own. I read a verse above him."

"That is well and good," Ulysses said. "That is as it should be. You did very well. But the body's gone."

"Gone! It can't be gone!" cried Enoch.

"It has been taken from the grave."

"But you can't know," protested Enoch. "How could you know?"

"Not I. It's the Vegans. The Vegans are the ones who know."

"But they're light-years distant . . ."

And then he was not too sure. For on that night the wise old one had died and he'd messaged Galactic Central, he had been told that the Vegans had known the moment he had died. And there had been no need for a death certificate, for they knew of what he died.

It seemed impossible, of course, but there were too many impossibilities in the galaxy which turned out, after all, to be entirely possible for a man to ever know when he stood on solid ground.

Was it possible, he wondered, that each Vegan had some sort of mental contact with every other Vegan? Or that some central census bureau (to give a human designation to something that was scarcely understandable) might have some sort of official linkage with every living Vegan, knowing where it was and how it was and what it might be doing?

Something of the sort, Enoch admitted, might indeed be possible. It was not beyond the astounding capabilities that one found on every hand throughout the galaxy. But to maintain a similar contact with the Vegan dead was something else again.

"The body's gone," Ulysses said. "I can tell you that and know it is the truth. You're held accountable."

"By the Vegans?"

"By the Vegans, yes. And the galaxy."

"I did what I could," said Enoch hotly. "I did what was required. I filled the letter of the Vegan law. I paid the dead my honor and the honor of my planet. It is not right that the responsibility should go on forever. Not that I can believe the body can be really gone. There is no one who would take it. No one who knew of it."

"By human logic," Ulysses told him, "you, of course, are right. But not by Vegan logic. And in this case Galactic Central would tend to support the Vegans."

"The Vegans," Enoch said testily, "happen to be friends of mine. I have never met a one of them that I didn't like or couldn't get along with. I can work it out with them."

"If only the Vegans were concerned," said Ulysses, "I am quite sure you could. I would have no worry. But the situation gets complicated as you go along. On the surface it seems a rather simple happening, but there are many factors. The Vegans, for example, have known for some time that the body had been taken and they were disturbed, of course. But out of certain considerations, they had kept their silence."

"They needn't have. They could have come to me. I don't know what could have been done . . ."

"Silent not because of you. Because of something else."

Ulysses finished off his coffee and poured himself another cup. He filled Enoch's half-filled cup and set the pot aside.

Enoch waited.

"You may not have been aware of it," said Ulysses, "but at the time this station was established, there was considerable opposition to it from a number of races in the galaxy. There were many reasons cited, as is the case in all such situations, but the underlying reason, when you get down to basics, rests squarely on the continual contest for racial or regional advantage. A situation akin, I would imagine, to the continual bickering and maneuvering which you find here upon the Earth to gain an economic advantage for one group or another, or one nation and another. In the galaxy, of course, the economic considerations only occasionally are the underlying factors. There are many other factors than the economic."

Enoch nodded. "I had gained a hint of this. Nothing recently. But I hadn't paid too much attention to it."

"It's largely a matter of direction," Ulysses said. "When Galactic Central began its expansion into this spiral arm, it meant there was no time or effort available for expansions in other directions. There is one large group of races which has held a dream for many centuries of expanding into some of the nearby globular clusters. It does make a dim sort of sense, of course. With the techniques that we have, the longer jump across space to some of the closer clusters is entirely possible. Another thing— the clusters seem to be extraordinarily free of dust and gas, so that once we got there we could expand more rapidly throughout the cluster than we can in many parts of the galaxy. But at best, it's a speculative business, for we don't know what we'll find there. After we've made all the effort and spent all the time we may find little or nothing, except possibly some more real estate. And we have plenty of that in the galaxy. But the clusters have a vast appeal for certain types of minds."

Enoch nodded. "I can see that. It would be the first venturing out of the galaxy itself. It might be the first short step on the route that could lead us to other galaxies."

Ulysses peered at him. "You, too," he said. "I might have known."

Enoch said smugly: "I am that type of mind."

"Well, anyhow, there was this globular-cluster faction—I suppose you'd call it that—which contended bitterly when we began our move in this direction. You understand—certainly you do—that we've barely begun the expansion into this neighborhood. We have less than a dozen stations and we'll need a hundred. It will take centuries before the network is complete."

"So this faction is still contending," Enoch said. "There still is time to stop this spiral-arm project."

"That is right. And that's what worries me. For the faction is set to use this incident of the missing body as an emotion-charged argument against the extension of this network. It is being joined by other groups that are concerned with certain special interests. And these special interest groups see a better chance of getting what they want if they can wreck this project."

"Wreck it?"

"Yes, wreck it. They will start screaming, as soon as the body incident becomes open knowledge, that a planet so barbaric as the Earth is no fit location for a station. They will insist that this station be abandoned."

"But they can't do that!"

"They can," Ulysses said. "They will say it is degrading and unsafe to maintain a station so barbaric that even graves are rifled, on a planet where the honored dead cannot rest in peace. It is the kind of highly emotional argument that will gain wide acceptance and support in some sections of the galaxy. The Vegans tried their best. They tried to hush it up, for the sake of the project. They have never done a thing like that before. They are a proud people and they feel a slight to honor—perhaps more deeply than many other races—and yet, for the greater good, they were willing to accept dishonor. And would have if they could have kept it quiet. But the story leaked out somehow—by good espionage, no doubt. And they cannot stand the loss of face in advertised dishonor. The Vegan who will be arriving here this evening is an official representative charged with delivering an official protest."

"To me?"

"To you, and through you, to the Earth."

"But the Earth is not concerned. The Earth doesn't even know."

"Of course it doesn't. So far as Galactic Central is concerned, you are the Earth. You represent the Earth."

Enoch shook his head. It was a crazy way of thinking. But, he told himself, he should not be surprised. It was the kind of thinking he should have expected. He was too hidebound, he thought, too narrow. He had been trained in the human way of thinking and, even after all these years, that way of thought persisted. Persisted to a point where any way of thought that conflicted with it must automatically seem wrong.

This talk of abandoning Earth station was wrong, too. It made no sort of sense. For abandoning of the station would not wreck the project. Although, more than likely, it would wreck whatever hope he'd held for the human race.

"But even if you have to abandon Earth," he said, "you could go out to Mars. You could build a station there. If it's necessary to have a station in this solar system there are other planets."

"You don't understand," Ulysses told him. "This station is just one point of attack. It is no more than a toehold, just a bare beginning. The aim is to wreck the project, to free the time and effort that is expended here for some other project. If they can force us to abandon one station, then we stand discredited. Then all our motives and our judgment come up for review."

"But even if the project should be wrecked," Enoch pointed out, "there is no surety that any group would gain. It would only throw the question of where the time and energy should be used into an open debate. You say that there are many special interest factions banding together to carry on the fight against us. Suppose that they do win. Then they must turn around and start fighting among themselves."

"Of course that's the case," Ulysses admitted, "but then each of them has a chance to get what they want, or think they have a chance. The way it is they have no chance at all. Before any of them has a chance this project must go down the drain. There is one group on the far side of the galaxy that wants to move out into the thinly populated sections of one particular section of the rim. They still believe in an ancient legend which says that their race arose as the result of immigrants from another galaxy who landed on the rim and worked their way inward over many galactic years. They think that if they can get out to the rim they can turn that legend into history to their greater glory. Another group wants to go into a small spiral arm because of an obscure record that many eons ago their ancestors picked up some virtually undecipherable messages which they believed came from that direction. Through the years the story has grown, until today they are convinced a race of intellectual giants will be found in that spiral arm. And there is always the pressure, naturally, to probe deeper into the galactic core. You must realize that we have only started, that the galaxy still is largely unexplored, that the thousands of races who form Galactic Central still are pioneers. And as a result, Galactic Central is continually subjected to all sorts of pressures."

"You sound," said Enoch, "as if you have little hope of maintaining this station, here on Earth."

"Almost no hope at all," Ulysses told him. "But so far as you yourself are concerned, there will be an option. You can stay here and live out an ordinary life on Earth or you can be assigned to another station. Galactic Central hopes that you would elect to continue on with us."

"That sounds pretty final."

"I am afraid," Ulysses said, "it is. I am sorry, Enoch, to be the bearer of bad news."

Enoch sat numb and stricken. Bad news! It was worse than that. It was the end of everything.

He sensed the crashing down of not only his own personal world, but of all the hopes of Earth. With the station gone, Earth once more would be left in the backwaters of the galaxy, with no hope of help, no chance of recognition, no realization of what lay waiting in the galaxy. Standing alone and naked, the human race would go on in its same old path, fumbling its uncertain way toward a blind, mad future.

20

The Hazer was elderly. The golden haze that enveloped him had lost the sparkle of its youthfulness. It was a mellow glow, deep and rich—not the blinding haze of a younger being. He carried himself with a solid dignity, and the flaring topknot that was neither hair nor feathers was white, a sort of saintly whiteness. His face was soft and tender, the softness and the tenderness which in a man might have been expressed in kindly wrinkles.

"I am sorry," he told Enoch, "that our meeting must be such as this. Although, under any circumstances, I am glad to meet you. I have heard of you. It is not often that a being of an outside planet is the keeper of a station. Because of this, young being, I have been intrigued with you. I have wondered what sort of creature you might turn out to be."

"You need have no apprehension of him," Ulysses said, a little sharply. "I will vouch for him. We have been friends for years."

"Yes, I forgot," the Hazer said. "You are his discoverer."

He peered around the room. "Another one," he said. "I did not know there were two of them. I only knew of one."

"It's a friend of Enoch's," Ulysses said.

"There has been contact, then. Contact with the planet."

"No, there has been no contact."

"Perhaps an indiscretion."

"Perhaps," Ulysses said, "but under provocation that I doubt either you or I could have stood against."

Lucy had risen to her feet and now she came across the room, moving quietly and slowly, as if she might be floating.

The Hazer spoke to her in the common tongue. "I am glad to meet you. Very glad to meet you."

"She cannot speak," Ulysses said. "Nor hear. She has no communication."

"Compensation," said the Hazer.

"You think so?" asked Ulysses.

"I am sure of it."

He walked slowly forward and Lucy waited.

"It—she, the female form, you called it—she is not afraid."

Ulysses chuckled. "Not even me," he said.

The Hazer reached out his hand to her and she stood quietly for a moment, then one of her hands came up and took the Hazer's fingers, more like tentacles than fingers, in its grasp.

It seemed to Enoch, for a moment, that the cloak of golden haze reached out to wrap the Earth girl in its glow. Enoch blinked his eyes and the illusion, if it had been illusion, was swept away, and it only was the Hazer who had the golden cloak.

And how was it, Enoch wondered, that there was no fear in her, either of Ulysses or the Hazer? Was it because, in truth, as he had said, she could see beyond the outward guise, could somehow sense the basic humanity (God help me, I cannot think, even now, except in human terms!) that was in these creatures? And if that were true, was it because she herself was not entirely human? A human, certainly, in form and origin, but not formed and molded into the human culture—being perhaps, what a human would be if he were not hemmed about so closely by the rules of behavior and outlook that through the years had hardened into law to comprise a common human attitude.

Lucy dropped the Hazer's hand and went back to the sofa.

The Hazer said, "Enoch Wallace."

"Yes."

"She is of your race?"

"Yes, of course she is."

"She is most unlike you. Almost as if there were two races."

"There is not two races. There is only one."

"Are there many others like her?"

"I would not know," said Enoch.

"Coffee," said Ulysses to the Hazer. "Would you like some coffee?"

"Coffee?"

"A most delicious brew. Earth's one great accomplishment."

"I am not acquainted with it," said the Hazer. "I don't believe I will."

He turned ponderously to Enoch.

"You know why I am here?" he asked.

"I believe so."

"It is a matter I regret," said the Hazer. "But I must . . ."

"If you'd rather," Enoch said, "we can consider that the protest has been made. I would so stipulate."

"Why not?" Ulysses said. "There is no need, it seems to me, to have the three of us go through a somewhat painful scene."

The Hazer hesitated.

"If you feel you must," said Enoch.

"No," the Hazer said. "I am satisfied if an unspoken protest be generously accepted."

"Accepted," Enoch said, "on just one condition. That I satisfy myself that the charge is not unfounded. I must go out and see."

"You do not believe me?"

"It is not a matter of belief. It is something that can be checked. I cannot accept either for myself or for my planet until I have done that much."

"Enoch," Ulysses said, "the Vegan has been gracious. Not only now, but before this happened. His race presses the charge most reluctantly. They suffered much to protect the Earth and you."

"And the feeling is that I would be ungracious if I did not accept the protest and the charge on the Vegan statement."

"I am sorry, Enoch," said Ulysses. "That is what I mean."

Enoch shook his head. "For years I've tried to understand and to conform to the ethics and ideas of all the people who have come through this station. I've pushed my own human instincts and training to one side. I've tried to understand other viewpoints and to evaluate other ways of thinking, many of which did violence to my own. I am glad of all of it, for it has given me a chance to go beyond the narrowness of Earth. I think I gained something from it all. But none of this touched Earth; only myself was involved. This business touches Earth and I must approach it from an Earthman's viewpoint. In this particular instance I am not simply the keeper of a galactic station."

Neither of them said a word. Enoch stood waiting and still there was nothing said.

Finally he turned and headed for the door.

"I'll be back," he told them.

He spoke the phrase and the door started to slide open.

"If you'll have me," said the Hazer quietly, "I'd like to go with you."

"Fine," said Enoch. "Come ahead."

It was dark outside and Enoch lit the lantern. The Hazer watched him closely.

"Fossil fuel," Enoch told him. "It burns at the tip of a saturated wick."

The Hazer said, in horror, "But surely you have better."

"Much better now," said Enoch. "I am just old-fashioned."

He led the way outside, the lantern throwing a small pool of light. The Hazer followed.

"It is a wild planet," said the Hazer.

"Wild here. There are parts of it are tame."

"My own planet is controlled," the Hazer said. "Every foot of it is planned."

"I know. I have talked to many Vegans. They described the planet to me."

They headed for the barn.

"You want to go back?" asked Enoch.

"No," said the Hazer. "I find it exhilarating. Those are wild plants over there?"

"We call them trees," said Enoch.

"The wind blows as it wishes?"

"That's right," said Enoch. "We do not know as yet how to control the weather."

The spade stood just inside the barn door and Enoch picked it up. He headed for the orchard.

"You know, of course," the Hazer said, "the body will be gone."

"I'm prepared to find it gone."

"Then why?" the Hazer asked.

"Because I must be sure. You can't understand that, can you?"

"You said back there in the station," the Hazer said, "that you tried to understand the rest of us. Perhaps, for a change, at least one of us should try understanding you."

Enoch led the way down the path through the orchard. They came to the rude fence enclosing the burial plot. The sagging gate stood open. Enoch went through it and the Hazer followed.

"This is where you buried him?"

"This is my family plot. My mother and my father are here and I put him with them."

He handed the lantern to the Vegan and, armed with the spade, walked up to the grave. He thrust the spade into the ground.

"Would you hold the lantern a little closer, please?"

The Hazer moved up a step or two.

Enoch dropped to his knees and brushed away the leaves that had fallen on the ground. Underneath them was the soft, fresh earth that had been newly turned. There was a depression and a small hole at the bottom of the depression. As he brushed at the earth, he could hear the clods of displaced dirt falling through the hole and striking on something that was not the soil.

The Hazer had moved the lantern again and he could not see. But he did not need to see. He knew there was no use of digging; he knew what he would find. He should have kept a watch. He should not have put up the stone to attract attention—but Galactic Central had said, "As if he were your own." And that was the way he'd done it.

He straightened, but remained upon his knees, felt the damp of the earth soaking through the fabric of his trousers.

"No one told me," said the Hazer, speaking softly.

"Told you what?"

"The memorial. And what is written on it. I was not aware that you knew our language."

"I learned it long ago. There were scrolls I wished to read. I'm afraid it's not too good."

"Two misspelled words," the Hazer told him, "and one little awkwardness. But those are things which do not matter. What matters, and matters very much, is that when you wrote, you thought as one of us."

Enoch rose and reached out for the lantern.

"Let's go back," he said sharply, almost impatiently. "I know now who did this. I have to hunt him out."

21

The treetops far above moaned in the rising wind. Ahead, the great clump of canoe birch showed whitely in the dim glow of the lantern's light. The birch clump, Enoch knew, grew on the lip of a small cliff that dropped twenty feet or more and here one turned to the right to get around it and continue down the hillside.

Enoch turned slightly and glanced over his shoulder. Lucy was following close behind. She smiled at him and made a gesture to say she was all right. He made a motion to indicate that they must turn to the right, that she must follow closely. Although, he told himself, it probably wasn't necessary; she knew the hillside as well, perhaps even better, than he did himself.

He turned to the right and followed along the edge of the rocky cliff, came to the break and clambered down to reach the slope below. Off to the left he could hear the murmur of the swiftly running creek that tumbled down the rocky ravine from the spring below the field.

The hillside plunged more steeply now and he led a way that angled across the steepness.

Funny, he thought, that even in the darkness he could recognize certain natural features—the crooked white oak that twisted itself, hanging at a crazy angle above the slope of hill; the small grove of massive red oaks that grew out of a dome of tumbled rock, so placed that no axman had even tried to cut them down; the tiny swamp, filled with cattails, that fitted itself snugly into a little terrace carved into the hillside.

Far below he caught the gleam of window light and angled down toward it. He looked back over his shoulder and Lucy was following close behind.

They came to a rude fence of poles and crawled through it and now the ground became more level.

Somewhere below a dog barked in the dark and another joined him. More joined in and the pack came sweeping up the slope toward them. They arrived in a rush of feet, veered around Enoch and the lantern to launch themselves at Lucy—suddenly transformed, at the sight of her, into a welcoming committee rather than a company of guards. They reared upward, a tangled mass of dogs. Her hands went out and patted at their heads. As if by signal, they went rushing off in a happy frolic, circling to come back again.

A short distance beyond the pole fence was a vegetable garden and Enoch led the way across, carefully following a path between the rows. Then they were in the yard and the house stood before them, a tumble-down, sagging structure, its outlines swallowed by the darkness, the kitchen windows glowing with a soft, warm lamplight.

Enoch crossed the yard to the kitchen door and knocked. He heard feet coming across the kitchen floor.

The door came open and Ma Fisher stood framed against the light, a great, tall, bony woman clothed in something that was more sack than dress.

She stared at Enoch, half frightened, half belligerent. Then, back of him, she saw the girl.

"Lucy!" she cried.

The girl came forward with a rush and her mother caught her in her arms.

Enoch set his lantern on the ground, tucked the rifle underneath his arm, and stepped across the threshold.

The family had been at supper, seated about a great round table set in the center of the kitchen. An ornate oil lamp stood in the center of the table. Hank had risen to his feet, but his three sons and the stranger still were seated.

"So you brung her back," said Hank.

"I found her," Enoch said.

"We quit hunting for her just a while ago," Hank told him. "We was going out again."

"You remember what you told me this afternoon?" asked Enoch.

"I told you a lot of things."

"You told me that I had the devil in me. Raise your hand against that girl once more and I promise you I'll show you just how much devil there is in me."

"You can't bluff me," Hank blustered.

But the man was frightened. It showed in the limpness of his face, the tightness of his body.

"I mean it," Enoch said. "Just try me out and see."

The two men stood for a moment, facing one another, then Hank sat down.

"Would you join us in some victuals?" he inquired.

Enoch shook his head.

He looked at the stranger. "Are you the ginseng man?" he asked.

The man nodded. "That is what they call me."

"I want to talk with you. Outside."

Claude Lewis stood up.

"You don't have to go," said Hank. "He can't make you go. He can talk to you right here."

"I don't mind," said Lewis. "In fact, I want to talk with him. You're Enoch Wallace, aren't you?"

"That's who he is," said Hank. "Should of died of old age fifty years ago. But look at him. He's got the devil in him. I tell you, him and the devil has a deal."

"Hank," Lewis said, "shut up."

Lewis came around the table and went out the door.

"Good night," Enoch said to the rest of them.

"Mr. Wallace," said Ma Fisher, "thanks for bringing back my girl. Hank won't hit her again. I can promise you. I'll see to that."

Enoch went outside and shut the door. He picked up the lantern. Lewis was out in the yard. Enoch went to him.

"Let's walk off a ways," he said.

They stopped at the edge of the garden and turned to face one another.

"You been watching me," said Enoch.

Lewis nodded.

"Official? Or just snooping?"

"Official, I'm afraid. My name is Claude Lewis. There is no reason I shouldn't tell you—I'm C.I.A."

"I'm not a traitor or a spy," Enoch said.

"No one thinks you are. We're just watching you."

"You know about the cemetery?"

Lewis nodded.

"You took something from a grave."

"Yes," said Lewis. "The one with the funny headstone."

"Where is it?"

"You mean the body. It's in Washington."

"You shouldn't have taken it," Enoch said, grimly. "You've caused a lot of trouble. You have to get it back. As quickly as you can."

"It will take a little time," said Lewis. "They'll have to fly it out. Twenty-four hours, maybe."

"That's the fastest you can make it."

"I might do a little better."

"Do the very best you can. It's important that you get that body back."

"I will, Wallace. I didn't know . . ."

"And, Lewis."

"Yes."

"Don't try to play it smart. Don't add any frills. Just do what I tell you. I'm trying to be reasonable because that's the only thing to be. But you try one smart move . . ."

He reached out a hand and grabbed Lewis's shirt front, twisting the fabric tight.

"You understand me, Lewis?"

Lewis was unmoved. He did not try to pull away.

"Yes," he said. "I understand."

"What the hell ever made you do it?"

"I had a job."

"Yeah, a job. Watching me. Not robbing graves."

He let loose of the shirt.

"Tell me," said Lewis, "that thing in the grave. What was it?"

"That's none of your damn' business," Enoch told him, bitterly. "Getting back that body is. You're sure that you can do it? Nothing standing in your way?"

Lewis shook his head. "Nothing at all. I'll phone as soon as I can reach a phone. I'll tell them that it's imperative."

"It's all of that," said Enoch. "Getting that body back is the most important thing you've ever done. Don't forget that for a minute. It affects everyone on Earth. You and me and everyone. And if you fail, you'll answer to me for it."

"With that gun?"

"Maybe," Enoch said. "Don't fool around. Don't imagine that I'd hesitate to kill you. In this situation, I'd kill anyone—anyone at all."

"Wallace, is there something you can tell me?"

"Not a thing," said Enoch.

He picked up the lantern.

"You're going home?"

Enoch nodded.

"You don't seem to mind us watching you."

"No," Enoch told him. "Not your watching. Just your interference. Bring back that body and go on watching if you want to. But don't push me any. Don't lean on me. Keep your hands off. Don't touch anything."

"But good God, man, there's something going on. You can tell me something."

Enoch hesitated.

"Some idea," said Lewis, "of what this is all about. Not the details, just . . ."

"You bring the body back," Enoch told him, slowly, "and maybe we can talk again."

"It will be back," said Lewis.

"If it's not," said Enoch, "you're as good as dead right now."

Turning, he went across the garden and started up the hill.

In the yard, Lewis stood for a long time, watching the lantern bobbing out of sight.

22

Ulysses was alone in the station when Enoch returned. He had sent the Thuban on his way and the Hazer back to Vega.

A fresh pot of coffee was brewing and Ulysses was sprawled out on the sofa, doing nothing.

Enoch hung up the rifle and blew out the lantern. Taking off his jacket, he threw it on the desk. He sat down in a chair across from the sofa.

"The body will be back," he said, "by this time tomorrow."

"I sincerely hope," Ulysses said, "that it will do some good. But I'm inclined to doubt it."

"Maybe," said Enoch bitterly, "I should not have bothered."

"It will show good faith," Ulysses said. "It might have some mitigating effect in the final weighing."

"The Hazer could have told me," Enoch said, "where the body was. If he knew it had been taken from the grave, then he must have known where it could be found."

"I would suspect he did," Ulysses said, "but, you see, he couldn't tell you. All that he could do was to make his protest. The rest was up to you. He could not lay aside his dignity by suggesting what you should do about it. For the record, he must remain the injured party."

"Sometimes," said Enoch, "this business is enough to drive one crazy. Despite the briefings from Galactic Central, there are always some surprises, always yawning traps for you to tumble into."

"There may come a day," Ulysses said, "when it won't be like that. I can look ahead and see, in some thousands of years, the knitting of the galaxy together into one great culture, one huge area of understanding. The local and the racial variations still will exist, of course, and that is as it should be, but overriding all of these will be a tolerance that will make for what one might be tempted to call a brotherhood."

"You sound," said Enoch, "almost like a human. That is the sort of hope that many of our thinkers have held out."

"Perhaps," Ulysses said. "You know that a lot of Earth seems to have rubbed off on me. You can't spend as long as I did on your planet without picking up at least a bit of it. And by the way, you made a good impression on the Vegan."

"I hadn't noticed it," Enoch told him. "He was kind and correct, of course, but little more."

"That inscription on the gravestone. He was impressed by that."

"I didn't put it there to impress anyone. I wrote it out because it was the way I felt. And because I like the Hazers. I was only trying to make it right for them."

"If it were not for the pressure from the galactic factions," Ulysses said, "I am convinced the Vegans would be willing to forget the incident and that is a greater concession than you can realize. It may be that, even so, they may line up with us when the showdown comes."

"You mean they might save the station?"

Ulysses shook his head. "I doubt anyone can do that. But it will be easier for all of us at Galactic Central if they threw their weight with us."

The coffeepot was making sounds and Enoch went to get it. Ulysses had pushed some of the trinkets on the coffee table to one side to make room for two coffee cups. Enoch filled them and set the pot upon the floor.

Ulysses picked up his cup, held it for a moment in his hands, then put it back on the table top.

"We're in bad shape," he said. "Not like in the old days. It has Galactic Central worried. All this squabbling and haggling among the races, all the pushing and the shoving."

He looked at Enoch. "You thought it was all nice and cozy."

"No," said Enoch, "not that. I knew that there were conflicting viewpoints and I knew there was some trouble. But I'm afraid I thought of it as being on a fairly lofty plane—gentlemanly, you know, and good-mannered."

"That was the way it was at one time. There always has been differing opinions, but they were based on principles and ethics, not on special interests. You know about the spiritual force, of course—the universal spiritual force."

Enoch nodded. "I've read some of the literature. I don't quite understand, but I'm willing to accept it. There is a way, I know, to get in contact with the force."

"The Talisman," said Ulysses.

"That's it. The Talisman. A machine, of sorts."

"I suppose," Ulysses agreed, "you could call it that. Although the word, "machine," is a little awkward. More than mechanics went into the making of it. There is just the one. Only one was ever made, by a mystic who lived ten thousand of your years ago. I wish I could tell you what it is or how it is constructed, but there is no one, I am afraid, who can tell you that. There have been others who have attempted to duplicate the Talisman, but no one has succeeded. The mystic who made it left no blueprints, no plans, no specifications, not a single note. There is no one who knows anything about it."

"There is no reason, I suppose," said Enoch, "that another should not be made. No sacred taboos, I mean. To make another one would not be sacrilegious."

"Not in the least," Ulysses told him. "In fact, we need another badly. For now we have no Talisman. It has disappeared."

Enoch jerked upright in his chair.

"Disappeared?" he asked.

"Lost," said Ulysses. "Misplaced. Stolen. No one knows."

"But I hadn't . . ."

Ulysses smiled bleakly. "You hadn't heard. I know. It is not something that we talk about. We wouldn't dare. The people must not know. Not for a while, at least."

"But how can you keep it from them?"

"Not too hard to do. You know how it worked, how the custodian took it from planet to planet and great mass meetings were held, where the Talisman was exhibited and contact made through it with the spiritual force. There had never been a schedule of appearances; the custodian simply wandered. It might be a hundred of your years or more between the visits of the custodian to any particular planet. The people hold no expectations of a visit. They simply know there'll be one, sometime; that some day the custodian will show up with the Talisman."

"That way you can cover up for years."

"Yes," Ulysses said. "Without any trouble."

"The leaders know, of course. The administrative people."

Ulysses shook his head. "We have told very few. The few that we can trust. Galactic Central knows, of course, but we're a close-mouthed lot."

"Then why . . ."

"Why should I be telling you. I know; I shouldn't. I don't know why I am. Yes, I guess I do. How does it feel, my friend, to sit as a compassionate confessor?"

"You're worried," Enoch said. "I never thought I would see you worried."

"It's a strange business," Ulysses said. "The Talisman has been missing for several years or so. And no one knows about it—except Galactic Central and the—what would you call it?—the hierarchy, I suppose, the organization of mystics who take care of the spiritual setup. And yet, even with no one knowing, the galaxy is beginning to show wear. It's coming apart at the seams. In time to come, it may fall apart. As if the Talisman represented a force that all unknowingly held the races of the galaxy together, exerting its influence even when it remained unseen."

"But even if it's lost, it's somewhere," Enoch pointed out.

"It still would be exerting its influence. It couldn't have been destroyed."

"You forget," Ulysses reminded him, "that without its proper custodian, without its sensitive, it is inoperative. For it's not the machine itself that does the trick. The machine merely acts as an intermediary between the sensitive and the spiritual force. It is an extension of the sensitive. It magnifies the capability of the sensitive and acts as a link of some sort. It enables the sensitive to perform his function."

"You feel that the loss of the Talisman has something to do with the situation here?"

"The Earth station. Well, not directly, but it is typical. What is happening in regard to the station is symptomatic. It involves the sort of petty quarreling and mean bickering that has broken out through many sections of the galaxy. In the old days it would have been—what did you say, gentlemanly and on a plane of principles and ethics."

They sat in silence for a moment, listening to the soft sound that the wind made as it blew through the gable gingerbread.

"Don't worry about it," Ulysses said. "It is not your worry. I should not have told you. It was indiscreet to do so."

"You mean I shouldn't pass it on. You can be sure I won't."

"I know you won't," Ulysses said. "I never thought you would."

"You really think relations in the galaxy are deteriorating?"

"Once," Ulysses said, "the races all were bound together. There were differences, naturally, but these differences were bridged, sometimes rather artificially and not too satisfactorily, but with both sides striving to maintain the artificial bridging and generally succeeding. Because they wanted to, you see. There was a common purpose, the forging of a great cofraternity of all intelligences. We realized that among us, among all the races, we had a staggering fund of knowledge and of techniques— that working together, by putting together all this knowledge and capability, we could arrive at something that would be far

greater and more significant than any race, alone, could hope of
accomplishing. We had our troubles, certainly, and as I have
said, our differences, but we were progressing. We brushed the
small animosities and the petty differences underneath the rug
and worked only on the big ones. We felt that if we could get
the big ones settled, the small ones would become so small they
would disappear. But it is becoming different now. There is a
tendency to pull the pettiness from underneath the rug and
blow it beyond its size, meanwhile letting the major and the
important issues fall away."

"It sounds like Earth," said Enoch.

"In many ways," Ulysses said. "In principle, although the
circumstances would diverge immensely."

"You've been reading the papers I have been saving for you?"

Ulysses nodded. "It doesn't look too happy."

"It looks like war," said Enoch bluntly.

Ulysses stirred uneasily.

"You don't have wars," said Enoch.

"The galaxy, you mean. No, as we are set up now we don't
have wars."

"Too civilized?"

"Stop being bitter," Ulysses told him. "There has been a
time or two when we came very close, but not in recent years.
There are many races now in the cofraternity that in their for-
mative years had a history of war."

"There is hope for us, then. It's something you outgrow."

"In time, perhaps."

"But not a certainty?"

"No, I wouldn't say so."

"I've been working on a chart," said Enoch. "Based on the
Mizar system of statistics. The chart says there is going to be
war."

"You don't need the chart," Ulysses said, "to tell you that."

"But there was something else. It was not just knowing if
there'd be a war. I had hoped that the chart might show how

to keep the peace. There must be a way. A formula, perhaps. If we could only think of it or know where to look or whom to ask or . . ."

"There is a way," Ulysses said, "to prevent a war."

"You mean you know . . ."

"It's a drastic measure. It only can be used as a last resort."

"And we've not reached that last resort?"

"I think, perhaps, you have. The kind of war that Earth would fight could spell an end to thousands of years of advancement, could wipe out all the culture, everything but the feeble remnants of civilizations. It could, just possibly, eliminate most of the life upon the planet."

"This method of yours—it has been used?"

"A few times."

"And worked?"

"Oh, certainly. We'd not even consider it if it didn't work."

"It could be used on Earth?"

"You could apply for its application."

"I?"

"As a representative of the Earth. You could appear before Galactic Central and appeal for us to use it. As a member of your race, you could give testimony and you would be given a hearing. If there seemed to be merit in your plea, Central might name a group to investigate and then, upon the report of its findings, a decision would be made."

"You said I. Could anyone on Earth?"

"Anyone who could gain a hearing. To gain a hearing, you must know about Galactic Central and you're the only man of Earth who does. Besides, you're a part of Galactic Central's staff. You have served as a keeper for a long time. Your record has been good. We would listen to you."

"But one man alone! One man can't speak for an entire race."

"You're the only one of your race who is qualified."

"If I could consult some others of my race."

"You can't. And even if you could, who would believe you?"

"That's true," said Enoch.

Of course it was. To him there was no longer any strangeness in the idea of a galactic cofraternity, of a transportation network that spread among the stars—a sense of wonder at times, but the strangeness had largely worn off. Although, he remembered, it had taken years. Years even with the physical evidence there before his eyes, before he could bring himself to a complete acceptance of it. But tell it to any other Earthman and it would sound like madness.

"And this method?" he asked, almost afraid to ask it, braced to take the shock of whatever it might be.

"Stupidity," Ulysses said.

Enoch gasped. "Stupidity? I don't understand. We are stupid enough, in many ways, right now."

"You're thinking of intellectual stupidity and there is plenty of that, not only on Earth, but throughout the galaxy. What I am talking about is a mental incapacity. An inability to understand the science and the technique that makes possible the kind of war that Earth would fight. An inability to operate the machines that are necessary to fight that kind of war. Turning the people back to a mental position where they would not be able to comprehend the mechanical and technological and scientific advances they have made. Those who know would forget. Those who didn't know could never learn. Back to the simplicity of the wheel and lever. That would make your kind of war impossible."

Enoch sat stiff and straight, unable to speak, gripped by an icy terror, while a million disconnected thoughts went chasing one another in a circle through his brain.

"I told you it was drastic," Ulysses said. "It has to be. War is something that costs a lot to stop. The price is high."

"I couldn't!" Enoch said. "No one could."

"Perhaps you can't. But consider this: If there is a war . . ."

"I know. If there is a war, it could be worse. But it wouldn't stop war. It's not the kind of thing I had in mind. People still could fight, still could kill."

"With clubs," said Ulysses. "Maybe bows and arrows. Rifles, so long as they still had rifles, and until they ran out of ammunition. Then they wouldn't know how to make more powder or how to get the metal to make the bullets or even how to make the bullets. There might be fighting, but there'd be no holocaust. Cities would not be wiped out by nuclear warheads, for no one could fire a rocket or arm the warhead—perhaps wouldn't even know what a rocket or a warhead was. Communications as you know them would be gone. All but the simplest transportation would be gone. War, except on a limited local scale, would be impossible."

"It would be terrible," Enoch said.

"So is war," Ulysses said. "The choice is up to you."

"But how long?" asked Enoch. "How long would it last? We wouldn't have to go back to stupidity forever?"

"Several generations," said Ulysses. "By that time the effect of—what shall we call it? the treatment?—would gradually begin wearing off. The people slowly would shake off their moronic state and begin their intellectual climb again. They'd be given, in effect, a second chance."

"They could," said Enoch, "in a few generations after that arrive at exactly the same situation that we have today."

"Possibly. I wouldn't expect it, though. Cultural development would be most unlikely to be entirely parallel. There'd be a chance that you'd have a better civilization and a more peaceful people."

"It's too much for one man . . ."

"Something hopeful," Ulysses said, "that you might consider. The method is offered only to those races which seem to us to be worth the saving."

"You have to give me time," said Enoch.

But he knew there was no time.

23

A man would have a job and suddenly be unable to perform it. Nor could the men around him carry on their jobs. For they would not have the knowledge or the backgrounds to do the tasks that they had been doing. They might try, of course —they might keep on trying for a time, but perhaps for not too long. And because the jobs could not be done, the business or the corporation or factory or whatever it might be, would cease its operation. Although the going out of business would not be a formal nor a legal thing. It would simply stop. And not entirely because the jobs could not be done, because no one could muster the business sense to keep it operating, but also because the transportation and communications which made the business possible also would have stopped.

Locomotives could not be operated, nor could planes and ships, for there would be no one who would remember how to operate them. There would be men who at one time had possessed all the skills that had been necessary for their operation, but now the skills would have disappeared. There might be some who still would try, with tragic consequences. And there still might be a few who could vaguely remember how to operate the car or truck or bus, for they were simple things to run and it would be almost second nature for a man to drive them. But once they had broken down, there would be no one with the knowledge of mechanics to repair them and they'd not run again.

In the space of a few hours' time the human race would be stranded in a world where distance once again had come to be a factor. The world would grow the larger and the oceans would be barriers and a mile would be long once more. And in a few days' time there would be a panic and a huddling and a fleeing and a desperation in the face of a situation that no one could comprehend.

How long, Enoch wondered, would it take a city to use the last of the food stacked in its warehouses and then begin to starve? What would happen when electricity stopped flowing through the wires? How long, under a situation such as this, would a silly symbolic piece of paper or a minted coin still retain its value?

Distribution would break down; commerce and industry would die; government would become a shadow, with neither the means nor the intelligence to keep it functioning; communications would cease; law and order would disintegrate; the world would sink into a new barbaric framework and would begin to slowly readjust. That readjustment would go on for years and in the process of it there would be death and pestilence and untold misery and despair. In time it would work out and the world would settle down to its new way of life, but in the process of shaking down there'd be many who would die and many others who would lose everything that had spelled out life for them and the purpose of that life.

But would it, bad as it might be, be as bad as war?

Many would die of cold and hunger and disease (for medicine would go the way of all the rest), but millions would not be annihilated in the fiery breath of nuclear reaction. There would be no poison dust raining from the skies and the waters still would be as pure and fresh as ever and the soil remain as fertile. There still would be a chance, once the initial phases of the change had passed, for the human race to go on living and rebuild society.

If one were certain, Enoch told himself, that there would be a war, that war was inescapable, then the choice might not be hard to make. But there was always the possibility that the world could avoid war, that somehow a frail, thin peace could be preserved, and in such a case the desperate need of the galactic cure for war would be unnecessary. Before one could decide, he told himself, one must be sure; and how could one be sure? The chart lying in the desk drawer said there would be a war; many of the diplomats and observers felt that the upcoming peace conference might serve no other purpose than to trigger war. Yet there was no surety.

And even if there were, Enoch asked himself, how could one man—one man, alone—take it upon himself to play the role of God for the entire race? By what right did one man make a decision that affected all the rest, all the billions of others? Could he, if he did, ever be able, in the years to come, to justify his choice?

How could a man decide how bad war might be and, in comparison, how bad stupidity? The answer seemed to be he couldn't. There was no way to measure possible disaster in either circumstance.

After a time, perhaps, a choice either way could be rationalized. Given time, a conviction might develop that would enable a man to arrive at some sort of decision which, while it might not be entirely right, he nevertheless could square with his conscience.

Enoch got to his feet and walked to the window. The sound of his footsteps echoed hollowly in the station. He looked at his watch and it was after midnight.

There were races in the galaxy, he thought, who could reach a quick and right decision on almost any question, cutting straight across all the tangled lines of thought, guided by rules of logic that were more specific than anything the human race might have. That would be good, of course, in the sense that it made decision possible, but in arriving at decision would it not tend to minimize, perhaps ignore entirely, some of those very facets of the situation that might mean more to the human race than the decision would itself?

Enoch stood at the window and stared out across the moonlit fields that ran down to the dark line of the woods. The clouds had blown away and the night was peaceful. This particular spot, he thought, always would be peaceful, for it was off the beaten track, distant from any possible target in atomic war. Except for the remote possibility of some ancient and non-recorded, long forgotten minor conflict in prehistoric days, no battle ever had been fought here or ever would be fought. And yet it could not escape the common fate of poisoned soil and water if the world should suddenly, in a fateful hour of fury, unleash the might of its awesome weapons. Then the skies would be filled with atomic ash, which would come sifting down, and it would make little difference where a man might be. Soon or late, the war would come to him, if not in a flash of monstrous energy, then in the snow of death falling from the skies.

He walked from the window to the desk and gathered up the newspapers that had come in the morning mail and put them in a pile, noticing as he did so that Ulysses had forgotten to take with him the stack of papers which had been saved for him. Ulysses was upset, he told himself, or he'd not have forgotten the papers. God save us both, he thought; for we have our troubles.

It had been a busy day. He had done no more, he realized, than read two or three of the stories in the *Times*, all touching on the calling of the conference. The day had been too full, too full of direful things.

For a hundred years, he thought, things had gone all right. There had been the good moments and the bad, but by and large his life had gone on serenely and without alarming incident. Then today had dawned and all the serene years had come tumbling down all about his ears.

There once had been a hope that Earth could be accepted as a member of the galactic family, that he might serve as the emissary to gain that recognition. But now that hope was shattered, not only by the fact that the station might be closed, but that its very closing would be based upon the barbarism of the human race. Earth was being used as a whipping boy, of course, in galactic politics, but the brand, once placed, could not soon be lifted. And in any event, even if it could be lifted, now the planet stood revealed as one against which Galactic Central, in the hope of saving it, might be willing to apply a drastic and degrading action.

There was something he could salvage out of all of it, he knew. He could remain an Earthman and turn over to the people of the Earth the information that he had gathered through the years and written down, in meticulous detail, along with personal happenings and impressions and much other trivia, in the long rows of record books which stood on the shelves against the wall. That and the alien literature he had obtained and read and hoarded. And the gadgets and the artifacts which came from other worlds. From all of this the people of the Earth might gain something which could help them along the road that eventually would take them to the stars and to that further knowledge and that greater understanding which would be their heritage—perhaps the heritage and right of all intelligence. But the wait for that day would be long—longer now, because of what had happened on this day, than it had ever been before. And the information that he held, gathered painfully over the course of almost a century, was so inadequate compared with that more complete knowledge which he could have gathered in another century (or a thousand years) that it seemed a pitiful thing to offer to his people.

If there could only be more time, he thought. But, of course, there never was. There was not the time right now and there would never be. No matter how many centuries he might be able to devote, there'd always be so much more knowledge than he'd gathered at the moment that the little he had gathered would always seem a pittance.

He sat down heavily in the chair before the desk and now, for the first time, he wondered how he'd do it—how he could leave Galactic Central, how he could trade the galaxy for a single planet, even if that planet still remained his own.

He drove his haggard mind to find the answer and the mind could find no answer.

One man alone, he thought.

One man alone could not stand against both Earth and galaxy.

24

The sun streaming through the window woke him and he stayed where he was, not stirring for a moment, soaking in its warmth. There was a good, hard feeling to the sunlight, a reassuring touch, and for a moment he held off the worry and the questioning. But he sensed its nearness and he closed his eyes again. Perhaps if he could sleep some more it might go away and lose itself somewhere and not be there when he awakened later.

But there was something wrong, something besides the worry and the questioning.

His neck and shoulders ached and there was a strange stiffness in his body and the pillow was too hard.

He opened his eyes again and pushed with his hands to sit erect and he was not in bed. He was sitting in a chair and his head, instead of resting on a pillow, had been laid upon the desk. He opened and shut his mouth to taste it, and it tasted just as bad as he knew it would.

He got slowly to his feet, straightening and stretching, trying to work out the kinks that had tied themselves into joints and muscles. As he stood there, the worry and the trouble and the dreadful need of answers seeped back into him, from wherever they'd been hiding. But he brushed them to one side, not an entirely successful brush, but enough to make them retreat a little and crouch there, waiting to close in again.

He went to the stove and looked for the coffeepot, then remembered that last night he'd set it on the floor beside the coffee table. He went to get it. The two cups still stood on the table, the dark brown dregs of coffee covering the bottoms of them. And in the mass of gadgets that Ulysses had pushed to one side to make room for the cups, the pyramid of spheres lay tilted on its side, but it still was sparkling and glinting, each successive sphere revolving in an opposite direction to its fellow spheres.

Enoch reached out and picked it up. His fingers carefully explored the base upon which the spheres were set, seeking something—some lever, some indentation, some trip, some button—by which it might be turned either on or off. But there was nothing he could find. He should have known, he told himself, that there would be nothing. For he had looked before. And yet yesterday Lucy had done something that had set it operating and it still was operating. It had operated for more than twelve hours now and no results had been obtained. Check that, he thought—no results that could be recognized.

He set it back on the table on its base and stacked the cups, one inside the other, and picked them up. He stooped to lift the coffeepot off the floor. But his eyes never left the pyramid of spheres.

It was maddening, he told himself. There was no way to turn it on and yet, somehow, Lucy had turned it on. And now there was no way to turn it off—although it probably did not matter if it were off or on.

He went back to the sink with the cups and coffeepot.

The station was quiet—a heavy, oppressive quietness; although, he told himself, the impression of oppressiveness probably was no more than his imagination.

He crossed the room to the message machine and the plate was blank. There had been no messages during the night. It was silly of him, he thought, to expect there would be, for if there were, the auditory signal would be functioning, would continue to sound off until he pushed the lever.

Was it possible, he wondered, that the station might already

have been abandoned, that whatever traffic that happened to
be moving was being detoured around it? That, however, was
hardly possible, for the abandonment of Earth station would
mean as well that those beyond it must also be abandoned.
There were no shortcuts in the network extending out into the
spiral arm to make rerouting possible. It was not unusual for
many hours, even for a day, to pass without any traffic. The
traffic was irregular and had no pattern to it. There were times
when scheduled arrivals had to be held up until there were
facilities to take care of them, and there were other times when
there would be none at all, when the equipment would sit idle,
as it was sitting now.

Jumpy, he thought. I am getting jumpy.

Before they closed the station, they would let him know.
Courtesy, if nothing else, would demand that they do that.

He went back to the stove and started the coffeepot. In the
refrigerator he found a package of mush made from a cereal
grown on one of the Draconian jungle worlds. He took it out,
then put it back again and took out the last two eggs of the
dozen that Wins, the mailman, had brought out from town a
week or so ago.

He glanced at his watch and saw that he had slept later than
he thought. It was almost time for his daily walk.

He put the skillet on the stove and spooned in a chunk of
butter. He waited for the butter to melt, then broke in the eggs.

Maybe, he thought, he'd not go on the walk today. Except
for a time or two when a blizzard had been raging, it would be
the first time he had ever missed his walk. But because he always
did it, he told himself, contentiously, was no sufficient reason that
he should always take it. He'd just skip the walk and later on
go down and get the mail. He could use the time to catch up on
all the things he'd failed to do yesterday. The papers still were
piled upon the desk, waiting for his reading. He'd not written
in his journal, and there was a lot to write, for he must record

in detail exactly what had happened and there had been a good deal happening.

It had been a rule he'd set himself from the first day that the station had begun its operation—that he never skimped the journal. He might be a little late at times in getting it all down, but the fact that he was late or that he was pressed for time had never made him put down one word less than he had felt might be required to tell all there was to tell.

He looked across the room at the long rows of record books that were crowded on the shelves and thought, with pride and satisfaction, of the completeness of that record. Almost a century of writing lay between the covers of those books and there was not a single day that he had ever skipped.

Here was his legacy, he thought; here was his bequest to the world; here would be his entrance fee back into the human race; here was all he'd seen and heard and thought for almost a hundred years of association with those alien peoples of the galaxy.

Looking at the rows of books, the questions that he had shoved aside came rushing in on him and this time there was no denying them. For a short space of time he had held them off, the little time he'd needed for his brain to clear, for his body to become alive again. He did not fight them now. He accepted them, for there was no dodging them.

He slid the eggs out of the skillet onto the waiting plate. He got the coffeepot and sat down to his breakfast.

He glanced at his watch again.

There still was time to go on his daily walk.

25

The ginseng man was waiting at the spring.

Enoch saw him while still some distance down the trail and wondered, with a quick flash of anger, if he might be waiting there to tell him that he could not return the body of the Hazer, that something had come up, that he had run into unexpected difficulties.

And thinking that, Enoch remembered how he'd threatened the night before to kill anyone who held up the return of the body. Perhaps, he told himself, it had not been smart to say that. Wondering whether he could bring himself to kill a man— not that it would be the first man he had ever killed. But that had been long ago and it had been a matter then of kill or being killed.

He shut his eyes for a second and once again could see that slope below him, with the long lines of men advancing through the drifting smoke, knowing that those men were climbing up the ridge for one purpose only, to kill himself and those others who were atop the ridge.

And that had not been the first time nor had it been the last, but all the years of killing boiled down in essence to that single moment—not the time that came after, but that long and terrible instant when he had watched the lines of men purposefully striding up the slope to kill him.

It had been in that moment that he had realized the insanity of war, the futile gesture that in time became all but meaningless, the unreasoning rage that must be nursed long beyond the memory of the incident that had caused the rage, the sheer illogic that one man, by death or misery, might prove a right or uphold a principle.

Somewhere, he thought, on the long backtrack of history, the human race had accepted an insanity for a principle and had persisted in it until today that insanity-turned-principle stood ready to wipe out, if not the race itself, at least all of those things, both material and immaterial, that had been fashioned as symbols of humanity through many hard-won centuries.

Lewis had been sitting on a fallen log and now, as Enoch neared, he rose.

"I waited for you here," he said. "I hope that you don't mind."

Enoch stepped across the spring.

"The body will be here sometime in early evening," Lewis said. "Washington will fly it out to Madison and truck it here from there."

Enoch nodded. "I am glad to hear that."

"They were insistent," Lewis said, "that I should ask you once again what the body is."

"I told you last night," said Enoch, "that I can't tell you anything. I wish I could. I've been figuring for years how to get it told, but there's no way of doing it."

"The body is something from off this Earth," said Lewis. "We are sure of that."

"You think so," Enoch said, not making it a question.

"And the house," said Lewis, "is something alien, too."

"The house," Enoch told him, shortly, "was built by my father."

"But something changed it," Lewis said. "It is not the way he built it."

"The years change things," said Enoch.

"Everything but you."

Enoch grinned at him. "So it bothers you," he said. "You figure it's indecent."

Lewis shook his head. "No, not indecent. Not really anything. After watching you for years, I've come to an acceptance of you and everything about you. No understanding, naturally, but complete acceptance. Sometimes I tell myself I'm crazy, but that's only momentary. I've tried not to bother you. I've worked to keep everything exactly as it was. And now that I've met you, I am glad that is the way it was. But we're going at this wrong. We're acting as if we were enemies, as if we were strange dogs—and that's not the way to do it. I think that the two of us may have a lot in common. There's something going on and I don't want to do a thing that will interfere with it."

"But you did," said Enoch. "You did the worst thing that you could when you took the body. If you'd sat down and planned how to do me harm, you couldn't have done worse. And not only me. Not really me, at all. It was the human race you harmed."

"I don't understand," said Lewis. "I'm sorry, but I don't understand. There was the writing on the stone . . ."

"That was my fault," said Enoch. "I should never have put up that stone. But at the time it seemed the thing to do. I didn't think that anyone would come snooping around and . . ."

"It was a friend of yours?"

"A friend of mine? Oh, you mean the body. Well, not actually. Not that particular person."

"Now that it's done," Lewis said, "I'm sorry."

"Sorry doesn't help," said Enoch.

"But isn't there something—isn't there anything that can be done about it? More than just bringing back the body?"

"Yes," Enoch told him, "there might be something. I might need some help."

"Tell me," Lewis said, quickly. "If it can be done . . ."

"I might need a truck," said Enoch. "To haul away some stuff. Records and other things like that. I might need it fast."

"I can have a truck," said Lewis. "I can have it waiting. And men to help you load."

"I might want to talk to someone in authority. High authority. The President. Secretary of State. Maybe the U.N. I don't know. I have to think it out. And not only would I need a way to talk to them, but some measure of assurance that they would listen to what I had to say."

"I'll arrange," said Lewis, "for mobile short-wave equipment. I'll have it standing by."

"And someone who will listen?"

"That's right," said Lewis. "Anyone you say."

"And one thing more."

"Anything," said Lewis.

"Forgetfulness," said Enoch. "Maybe I won't need any of these things. Not the truck or any of the rest of it. Maybe I'll have to let things go just as they're going now. And if that should be the case, could you and everyone else concerned forget I ever asked?"

"I think we could," said Lewis. "But I would keep on watching."

"I wish you would," said Enoch. "Later on I might need some help. But no further interference."

"Are you sure," asked Lewis, "that there is nothing else?"

Enoch shook his head. "Nothing else. All the rest of it I must do myself."

Perhaps, he thought, he'd already talked too much. For how could he be sure that he could trust this man? How could he be sure he could trust anyone?

And yet, if he decided to leave Galactic Central and cast his lot with Earth, he might need some help. There might be some objection by the aliens to his taking along his records and the alien gadgets. If he wanted to get away with them, he might have to make it fast.

But did he want to leave Galactic Central? Could he give up the galaxy? Could he turn down the offer to become the keeper of another station on some other planet? When the time should come, could he cut his tie with all the other races and all the mysteries of the other stars?

Already he had taken steps to do those very things. Here, in the last few moments, without too much thought about it, almost as if he already had reached his decision, he had arranged a setup that would turn him back to Earth.

He stood there, thinking, puzzled at the steps he'd taken.

"There'll be someone here," said Lewis. "Someone at this spring. If not myself, then someone else who can get in touch with me."

Enoch nodded absent-mindedly.

"Someone will see you every morning when you take your walk," said Lewis. "Or you can reach us here any time you wish."

Like a conspiracy, thought Enoch. Like a bunch of kids playing cops and robbers.

"I have to be getting on," he said. "It's almost time for mail. Wins will be wondering what has happened to me."

He started up the hill.

"Be seeing you," said Lewis.

"Yeah," said Enoch. "I'll be seeing you."

He was surprised to find the warm glow spreading in him—as if there had been something wrong and now it was all right, as if there had been something lost that now had been recovered.

26

Enoch met the mailman halfway down the road that led into the station. The old jalopy was traveling fast, bumping over the grassy ruts, swishing through the overhanging bushes that grew along the track.

Wins braked to a halt when he caught sight of Enoch and sat waiting for him.

"You got on a detour," Enoch said, coming up to him. "Or have you changed your route?"

"You weren't waiting at the box," said Wins, "and I had to see you."

"Some important mail?"

"Nope, it isn't mail. It's old Hank Fisher. He is down in Millville, setting up the drinks in Eddie's tavern and shooting off his face."

"It's not like Hank to be buying drinks."

"He's telling everyone that you tried to kidnap Lucy."

"I didn't kidnap her," Enoch said. "Hank had took a bull whip to her and I hid her out until he got cooled down."

"You shouldn't have done that, Enoch."

"Maybe. But Hank was set on giving her a beating. He already had hit her a lick or two."

"Hank's out to make you trouble."

"He told me that he would."

"He says you kidnaped her, then got scared and brought her back. He says you had her hid out in the house and when he tried to break in and get her, he couldn't do it. He says you have a funny sort of house. He says he broke an ax blade on a window pane."

"Nothing funny about it," Enoch said. "Hank just imagines things."

"It's all right so far," said the mailman. "None of them, in broad daylight and their right senses, will do anything about it. But come night they'll be liquored up and won't have good sense. There are some of them might be coming up to see you."

"I suppose he's telling them I've got the devil in me."

"That and more," said Wins. "I listened for a while before I started out."

He reached into the mail pouch and found the bundle of papers and handed them to Enoch.

"Enoch, there's something that you have to know. Something you may not realize. It would be easy to get a lot of people stirred up against you—the way you live and all. You are strange. No, I don't mean there's anything wrong with you—I know you and I know there isn't—but it would be easy for people who didn't know you to get the wrong ideas. They've let you alone so far because you've given them no reason to do anything about you. But if they get stirred up by all that Hank is saying . . ."

He did not finish what he was saying. He left it hanging in midair.

"You're talking about a posse," Enoch said.

Wins nodded, saying nothing.

"Thanks," said Enoch. "I appreciate your warning me."

"Is it true," asked the mailman, "that no one can get inside your house?"

"I guess it is," admitted Enoch. "They can't break into it and they can't burn it down. They can't do anything about it."

"Then, if I were you, I'd stay close tonight. I'd stay inside. I'd not go venturing out."

"Maybe I will. It sounds like a good idea."

"Well," said Wins, "I guess that about covers it. I thought you'd ought to know. Guess I'll have to back out to the road. No chance of turning around."

"Drive up to the house. There's room there."

"It's not far back to the road," said Wins. "I can make it easy."

The car started backing slowly.

Enoch stood watching.

He lifted a hand in solemn salute as the car began rounding a bend that would take it out of sight. Wins waved back and then the car was swallowed by the scrub that grew close against both sides of the road.

Slowly Enoch turned around and plodded back toward the station.

A mob, he thought—good God, a mob!

A mob howling about the station, hammering at the doors and windows, peppering it with bullets, would wipe out the last faint chance—if there still remained a chance—of Galactic Central standing off the move to close the station. Such a demonstration would add one more powerful argument to the demand that the expansion into the spiral arm should be abandoned.

Why was it, he wondered, that everything should happen all at once? For years nothing at all had happened and now everything was happening within a few hours' time. Everything, it seemed, was working out against him.

If the mob showed up, not only would it mean that the fate of the station would be sealed, but it might mean, as well, that he would have no choice but to accept the offer to become the keeper of another station. It might make it impossible for him to remain on Earth, even if he wished. And he realized, with a start, that it might just possibly mean that the offer of another station for him might be withdrawn. For with the appearance of a mob howling for his blood, he, himself, would become involved in the charge of barbarism now leveled against the human race in general.

Perhaps, he told himself, he should go down to the spring and see Lewis once again. Perhaps some measures could be taken to hold off the mob. But if he did, he knew, there'd be an explanation due and he might have to tell too much. And there might not be a mob. No one would place too much credence in what Hank Fisher said and the whole thing might peter out without any action being taken.

He'd stay inside the station and hope for the best. Perhaps there'd be no traveler in the station at the time the mob arrived— if it did arrive—and the incident would pass with no galactic notice. If he were lucky it might work out that way. And by the law of averages, he was owed some luck. Certainly he'd had none in the last few days.

He came to the broken gate that led into the yard and stopped to look up at the house, trying, for some reason he could not understand, to see it as the house he had known in boyhood.

It stood the same as it had always stood, unchanged, except that in the olden days there had been ruffled curtains at each window. The yard around it had changed with the slow growth of the years, with the clump of lilacs thicker and more rank and tangled with each passing spring, with the elms that his father had planted grown from six-foot whips into mighty trees, with the yellow rose bush at the kitchen corner gone, victim of a long-forgotten winter, with the flower beds vanished and the small herb garden, here beside the gate, overgrown and smothered out by grass.

The old stone fence that had stood on each side of the gate now was little more than a humpbacked mound. The heaving of a hundred frosts, the creep of vines and grasses, the long years of neglect, had done their work and in another hundred years, he thought, it would be level, with no trace of it left. Down in the field, along the slope where erosion had been at work, there were long stretches where it had entirely disappeared.

All of this had happened and until this moment he had scarcely noticed it. But now he noticed it and wondered why he did. Was it because he now might be returning to the Earth again—he who had never left its soil and sun and air, who had never left it physically, but who had, for a longer time than most men had allotted to them, walked not one, but many planets, far among the stars?

He stood there, in the late summer sun, and shivered in the cold wind that seemed to be blowing out of some unknown dimension of unreality, wondering for the first time (for the first time he ever had been forced to wonder at it) what kind of man he was. A haunted man who must spend his days neither completely alien nor completely human, with divided loyalties, with old ghosts to tramp the years and miles with him no matter which life he might choose, the Earth life or the stars? A cultural half-breed, understanding neither Earth nor stars, owing a debt to each, but paying neither one? A homeless, footless, wandering creature who could recognize neither right nor wrong from having seen so many different (and logical) versions of the right and wrong?

He had climbed the hill above the spring, filled with the rosy inner glow of a regained humanity, a member of the human race again, linked in a boylike conspiracy with a human team. But could he qualify as human—and if he qualified as human, or tried to qualify, then what about the implied hundred years' allegiance to Galactic Central? Did he, he wondered, even want to qualify as human?

He moved slowly through the gate, and the questions still kept hammering in his brain, that great, ceaseless flow of questions to which there were no answers. Although that was wrong, he thought. Not no answers, but too many answers.

Perhaps Mary and David and the rest of them would come visiting tonight and they could talk it over—then he suddenly remembered.

They would not be coming. Not Mary, not David, nor any of the others. They had come for years to see him, but they would come no longer, for the magic had been dimmed and the illusion shattered and he was alone.

As he had always been alone, he told himself, with a bitter taste inside his brain. It all had been illusion; it never had been real. For years he'd fooled himself—most eagerly and willingly he had fooled himself into peopling the little corner by the fire-place with these creatures of his imagination. Aided by an alien technique, driven by his loneliness for the sight and sound of humankind, he had brought them into a being that defied every sense except the solid sense of touch.

And defied as well every sense of decency.

Half-creatures, he thought. Poor pitiful half-creatures, neither of the shadow or the world.

Too human for the shadows, too shadowy for Earth.

Mary, if I had only known—if I had known, I never would have started. I'd have stayed with loneliness.

And he could not mend it now. There was nothing that would help.

What is the matter with me? he asked himself.

What has happened to me?

What is going on?

He couldn't even think in a straight line any more. He'd told himself that he'd stay inside the station to escape the mob that might be showing up—and he couldn't stay inside the station, for Lewis, sometime shortly after dark, would be bringing back the Hazer's body.

And if the mob showed up at the same time Lewis should appear, bringing back the body, there'd be unsheeted hell to pay.

Stricken by the thought, he stood undecided.

If he alerted Lewis to the danger, then he might not bring the body. And he had to bring the body. Before the night was over the Hazer must be secure within the grave.

He decided that he would have to take a chance.

The mob might not show up. Even if it did, there had to be a way that he could handle it.

He'd think of something, he told himself.

He'd have to think of something.

27

The station was as silent as it had been when he'd left it. There had been no messages and the machinery was quiet, not even muttering to itself, as it sometimes did.

Enoch laid the rifle across the desk top and dropped the bundle of papers beside it. He took off his jacket and hung it on the back of the chair.

There were still the papers to be read, not only today's, but yesterday's as well, and the journal to be gotten up, and the journal, he reminded himself, would take a lot of time. There would be several pages of it, even if he wrote it close, and he must write it logically and chronologically, so that it would appear he had written the happenings of yesterday yesterday and not a full day late. He must include each event and every facet of each happening and his own reactions to it and his thoughts about it. For that was the way he'd always done and that was the way he must do it now. He'd always been able to do it that way because he had created for himself a little special niche, not of the Earth, nor of the galaxy, but in that vague condition which one might call existence, and he had worked inside the framework of that special niche as a medieval monk had worked inside his cell. He had been an observer only, an intensely interested observer who had not been content with observance only, but who had made an effort to dig into what he had observed, but still basically and essentially an observer who was not vitally nor personally involved in what had gone on about him. But in the last two days, he realized, he had lost that observer status. The Earth and the galaxy had both intruded on him, and his special niche was gone and he was personally involved. He had lost his objective viewpoint and no longer could command that correct and coldly factual approach which had given him a solid basis upon which to do his writing.

He walked over to the shelf of journals and pulled out the current volume, fluttering its pages to find where he had stopped. He found the place and it was very near the end. There were only a few blank pages left, perhaps not enough of them to cover the events of which he'd have to write. More than likely, he thought, he'd come to an end of the journal before he had finished with it and would have to start a new one.

He stood with the journal in his hand and stared at the page where the writing ended, the writing that he'd done the day before yesterday. Just the day before yesterday and it now was ancient writing; it even had a faded look about it. And well it might, he thought, for it had been writing done in another age. It had been the last entry he had made before his world had come crashing down about him.

And what, he asked himself, was the use of writing further? The writing now was done, all the writing that would matter. The station would be closed and his own planet would be lost— no matter whether he stayed on or went to another station on another planet, the Earth would now be lost.

Angrily he slammed shut the book and put it back into its place upon the shelf. He walked back to the desk.

The Earth was lost, he thought, and he was lost as well, lost and angry and confused. Angry at fate (if there were such a thing as fate) and at stupidity. Not only the intellectual stupidity of the Earth, but at the intellectual stupidity of the galaxy as well, at the petty bickering which could still the march of the brotherhood of peoples that finally had extended into this galactic sector. As on Earth, so in the galaxy, the number and complexity of the gadget, the noble thought, the wisdom and erudition might make for a culture, but not for a civilization. To be truly civilized, there must be something far more subtle than the gadget or the thought.

He felt the tension in him, the tension to be doing something —to prowl about the station like a caged and pacing beast, to run outside and shout incoherently until his lungs were empty, to smash and break, to work off, somehow, his rage and disappointment.

He reached out a hand and snatched the rifle off the desk. He pulled out a desk drawer where he kept the ammunition, and took out a box of it, tearing it apart, emptying the cartridges in his pocket.

He stood there for a moment, with the rifle in his hand, and the silence of the room seemed to thunder at him and he caught the bleakness and the coldness of it and he laid the rifle back on the desk again.

What childishness, he thought, to take out his resentment and his rage on an unreality. And when there was no real reason for resentment or for rage. For the pattern of events was one that should be recognized and thus accepted. It was the kind of thing to which a human being should long since have become accustomed.

He looked around the station and the quietness and the waiting still was there, as if the very structure might be marking time for an event to come along on the natural flow of time.

He laughed softly and reached for the rifle once again.

Unreality or not, it would be something to occupy his mind, to snatch him for a while from this sea of problems which was swirling all about him.

And he needed the target practice. It had been ten days or more since he'd been on the rifle range.

28

The basement was huge. It stretched out into a dim haze beyond the lights which he had turned on, a place of tunnels and rooms, carved deep into the rock that folded up to underlie the ridge.

Here were the massive tanks filled with the various solutions for the tank travelers; here the pumps and the generators, which operated on a principle alien to the human manner of generating electric power, and far beneath the floor of the basement itself those great storage tanks which held the acids and the soupy matter which once had been the bodies of those creatures which came traveling to the station, leaving behind them, as they went on to some other place, the useless bodies which then must be disposed of.

Enoch moved across the floor, past the tanks and generators, until he came to a gallery that stretched out into the darkness. He found the panel and pressed it to bring on the lights, then walked down the gallery. On either side were metal shelves which had been installed to accommodate the overflow of gadgets, of artifacts, of all sorts of gifts which had been brought him by the travelers. From floor to ceiling the shelves were jammed with a junkyard accumulation from all the corners of the galaxy. And yet, thought Enoch, perhaps not actually a junkyard, for there would be very little of this stuff that would be actual junk. All of it was serviceable and had some purpose, either practical or aesthetic, if only that purpose could be learned. Although perhaps not in every instance a purpose that would be applicable to humans.

Down at the end of the shelves was one section of shelving into which the articles were packed more systematically and with greater care, each one tagged and numbered, with cross-filing to a card catalogue and certain journal dates. These were the articles of which he knew the purpose and, in certain instances, something of the principles involved. There were some that were innocent enough and others that held great potential value and still others that had, at the moment, no connection whatsoever with the human way of life—and there were, as well, those few, tagged in red, that made one shudder to even think upon.

He went down the gallery, his footsteps echoing loudly as he trod through this place of alien ghosts.

Finally the gallery widened into an oval room and the walls here were padded with a thick gray substance that would entrap a bullet and prevent a ricochet.

Enoch walked over to a panel set inside a deep recess sunk into the wall. He reached in and thumbed up a tumbler, then stepped quickly out into the center of the room.

Slowly the room began to darken, then suddenly it seemed to flare and he was in the room no longer, but in another place, a place he had never seen before.

He stood on a little hillock and in front of him the land sloped down to a sluggish river bordered by a width of marsh. Between the beginning of the marsh and the foot of the hillock stretched a sea of rough, tall grass. There was no wind, but the grass was rippling and he knew that the rippling motion of the grass was caused by many moving bodies, foraging in the grass. Out of it came a savage grunting, as if a thousand angry hogs were fighting for choice morsels in a hundred swill troughs. And from somewhere farther off, perhaps from the river, came a deep, monotonous bellowing that sounded hoarse and tired.

Enoch felt the hair crawling on his scalp and he thrust the rifle out and ready. It was puzzling. He felt and knew the danger and as yet there was no danger. Still, the very air of this place— wherever it might be—seemed to crawl with danger.

He spun around and saw that close behind him the thick, dark woods climbed down the range of river hills, stopping at the sea of grass which flowed around the hillock on which he found himself. Off beyond the hills, dark purple in the air, loomed a range of mighty mountains that seemed to fade into the sky, but purple to their peaks, with no sign of snow upon them.

Two things came trotting from the woods and stopped at the edge of it. They sat down and grinned at him, with their tails wrapped neatly round their feet. They might have been wolves or dogs, but they were neither one. They were nothing he had ever seen or heard of. Their pelts glistened in the weak sun- shine, as if they had been greased, but the pelts stopped at their necks, with their skulls and faces bare. Like evil old men, off on a masquerade, with their bodies draped in the hides of wolves. But the disguise was spoiled by the lolling tongues which spilled out of their mouths, glistening scarlet against the bone-white of their faces.

The woods was still. There were only the two gaunt beasts sitting on their haunches. They sat and grinned at him, a strangely toothless grin.

The woods was dark and tangled, the foliage so dark green that it was almost black. All the leaves had a shine to them, as if they had been polished to a special sheen.

Enoch spun around again, to look back towards the river, and crouched at the edge of the grass was a line of toadlike mon- strosities, six feet long and standing three feet high, their bodies the color of a dead fish belly, and each with a single eye, or what seemed to be an eye, which covered a great part of the area just above the snout. The eyes were faceted and glowed in the dim sunlight, as the eyes of a hunting cat will glow when caught in a beam of light.

The hoarse bellowing still came from the river and in between the bellowing there was a faint, thin buzzing, an angry and malicious buzzing, as if a mosquito might be hovering for attack, although there was a sharper tone in it than in the noise of a mosquito.

Enoch jerked up his head to look into the sky and far in the depths of it he saw a string of dots, so high that there was no way of knowing what kind of things they were.

He lowered his head to look back at the line of squatting, toadlike things, but from the corner of his eye he caught the sense of flowing motion and swung back toward the woods.

The wolf-like bodies with the skull-like heads were coming up the hill in a silent rush. They did not seem to run. There was no motion of their running. Rather they were moving as if they had been squirted from a tube.

Enoch jerked up his rifle and it came into his shoulder, fitting there, as if it were a part of him. The bead settled in the rear-sight notch and blotted out the skull-like face of the leading beast. The gun bucked as he squeezed the trigger and, without waiting to see if the shot had downed the beast, the rifle barrel was swinging toward the second as his right fist worked the bolt. The rifle bucked again and the second wolf-like being somer-saulted and slid forward for an instant, then began rolling down the hill, flopping as it rolled.

Enoch worked the bolt again and the spent brass case glittered in the sun as he turned swiftly to face the other slope.

The toadlike things were closer now. They had been creeping in, but as he turned they stopped and squatted, staring at him.

He reached a hand into his pocket and took out two cartridges, cramming them into the magazine to replace the shells he'd fired.

The bellowing down by the river had stopped, but now there was a honking sound that he could not place. Turning cautiously, he tried to locate what might be making it, but there was nothing to be seen. The honking sound seemed to be coming from the forest, but there was nothing moving.

In between the honking, he still could hear the buzzing and it seemed louder now. He glanced into the sky and the dots were larger and no longer in a line. They had formed into a circle and seemed to be spiraling downward, but they were still so high that he could not make out what kinds of things they were.

He glanced back toward the toadlike monsters and they were closer than they had been before. They had crept up again.

Enoch lifted the rifle and, before it reached his shoulder, pressed the trigger, shooting from the hip. The eye of one of the foremost of them exploded, like the splash a stone would make if thrown into water. The creature did not jump or flop. It simply settled down, flat upon the ground, as if someone had put his foot upon it and had exerted exactly force enough to squash it flat. It lay there, flat, and there was a big round hole where the eye had been and the hole was filling with a thick and ropy yellow fluid that may have been the creature's blood.

The others backed away, slowly, watchfully. They backed all the way off the hillock and only stopped when they reached the grass edge.

The honking was closer and the buzzing louder and there could be no doubt that the honking was coming from the hills.

Enoch swung about and saw it, striding through the sky, coming down the ridge, stepping through the trees and honking dolefully. It was a round and black balloon that swelled and deflated with its honking, and jerked and swayed as it walked along, hung from the center of four stiff and spindly legs that arched above it to the joint that connected this upper portion of the leg arrangement with the downward-spraddling legs that raised it high above the forest. It was walking jerkily, lifting its legs high to clear the massive treetops before putting them down again. Each time it put down a foot, Enoch could hear the crunching of the branches and the crashing of the trees that it broke or brushed aside.

Enoch felt the skin along his spine trying to roll up his back like a window shade, and the bristling of the hair along the base of his skull, obeying some primordial instinct in its striving to raise itself erect into a fighting ruff.

But even as he stood there, almost stiff with fright, some part of his brain remembered that one shot he had fired and his fingers dug into his pocket for another cartridge to fill the magazine.

The buzzing was much louder and the pitch had changed. The buzzing was now approaching at tremendous speed.

Enoch jerked up his head and the dots no longer were circling in the sky, but were plunging down toward him, one behind the other.

He flicked a glance toward the balloon, honking and jerking on its stiltlike legs. It still was coming on, but the plunging dots were faster and would reach the hillock first.

He shifted the rifle forward, outstretched and ready to slap against his shoulder, and watched the falling dots, which were dots no longer, but hideous streamlined bodies, each carrying a rapier that projected from its head. A bill of sorts, thought Enoch, for these things might be birds, but a longer, thinner, larger, more deadly bird than any earthly bird.

The buzzing changed into a scream and the scream kept mounting up the scale until it set the teeth on edge and through it, like a metronome measuring off a beat, came the hooting of the black balloon that strode across the hills.

Without knowing that he had moved his arms, Enoch had the rifle at his shoulder, waiting for that instant when the first of the plunging monsters was close enough to fire.

They dropped like stones out of the sky and they were bigger than he had thought they were—big and coming like so many arrows aimed directly at him.

The rifle thudded against his shoulder and the first one

crumpled, lost its arrow shape, folding up and falling, no longer on its course. He worked the bolt and fired again and the second one in line lost its balance and began to tumble—and the bolt was worked once more and the trigger pressed. The third skidded in the air and went off at a slant, limp and ragged, fluttering in the wind, falling toward the river.

The rest broke off their dive. They made a shallow turn and beat their way up into the sky, great wings that were more like windmill vanes than wings thrashing desperately.

A shadow fell across the hillock and a mighty pillar came down from somewhere overhead, driving down to strike to one side of the hillock. The ground trembled at the tread and the water that lay hidden by the grass squirted high into the air.

The honking was an engulfing sound that blotted out all else and the great balloon was zooming down, cradled on its legs.

Enoch saw the face, if anything so grotesque and so obscene could be called a face. There was a beak and beneath it a sucking mouth and a dozen or so other organs that might have been the eyes.

The legs were like inverted V's, with the inner stroke somewhat shorter than the outer and in the center of these inner joints hung the great balloon that was the body of the creature, with its face on the underside so that it could see all the hunting territory that might lie beneath it.

But now auxiliary joints in the outer span of legs were bending to let the body of the creature down so it could seize its prey.

Enoch was not conscious of putting up the rifle or of operating it, but it was hammering at his shoulder and it seemed to him that a second part of him stood off, apart, and watched the firing of the rifle—as if the figure that held and fired the weapon might be a second man.

Great gouts of flesh flew out of the black balloon and jagged rents suddenly tore across it and from these rents poured out a cloud of liquid that turned into a mist, with black droplets raining from it.

The firing pin clicked on an empty breech and the gun was empty, but there was no need of another shot. The great legs were folding, and trembling as they folded, and the shrunken body shivered convulsively in the heavy mist that was pouring out of it. There was no hooting now, and Enoch could hear the patter of the black drops falling from that cloud as they struck the short grass on the hill.

There was a sickening odor and the drops, where they fell on him, were sticky, running like cold oil, and above him the great structure that had been the stiltlike creature was toppling to the ground.

Then the world faded swiftly and was no longer there.

Enoch stood in the oval room in the faint glow of the bulbs. There was the heavy smell of powder and all about his feet, glinting in the light, lay the spent and shining cases that had been kicked out of the gun.

He was back in the basement once again. The target shoot was over.

29

Enoch lowered the rifle and drew in a slow and careful breath. It always was like this, he thought. As if it were necessary for him to ease himself, by slow degrees, back to this world of his after the season of unreality.

One knew that it would be illusion when he kicked on the switch that set into motion whatever was to happen and one knew it had been illusion when it all had ended, but during the time that it was happening it was not illusion. It was as real and as substantial as if it all were true.

They had asked him, he remembered, when the station had been built, if he had a hobby—if there was any sort of recreational facility they could build into the station for him. And he had said that he would like a rifle range, expecting no more than a shooting gallery with ducks moving on a chain or clay pipes rotating on a wheel. But that, of course, would have been too simple for the screwball architects, who had designed, and the slap-happy crew of workmen who had built the station.

At first they had not been certain what he meant by a rifle range and he'd had to tell them what a rifle was and how it operated and for what it might be used. He had told them about hunting squirrels on sunny autumn mornings and shaking rabbits out of brush piles with the first coming of the snow (although one did not use a rifle, but a shotgun, on the rabbits), about hunting coons of an autumn night, and waiting for the deer along the run that went down to the river. But he was dishonest and he did not tell them about that other use to which he'd put a rifle during four long years.

He'd told them (since they were easy folks to talk with) about his youthful dream of some day going on a hunt in Africa, although even as he told them he was well aware of how unattainable it was. But since that day he'd hunted (and been hunted by) beasts far stranger than anything that Africa could boast.

From what these beasts might have been patterned, if indeed they came from anywhere other than the imagination of those aliens who had set up the tapes which produced the target scene, he had no idea. There had not, so far in the thousands of times that he had used the range, been a duplication either in the scene nor in the beasts which rampaged about the scene. Although, perhaps, he thought, there might be somewhere an end of them, and then the whole sequence might start over and run its course once more. But it would make little difference now, for if the tapes should start rerunning there'd be but little chance of his recalling in any considerable detail those adventures he had lived so many years ago.

He did not understand the techniques nor the principle which made possible this fantastic rifle range. Like many other things, he accepted it without the need of understanding. Although, some day, he thought, he might find the clue which in time would turn blind acceptance into understanding—not only of the range, but of many other things.

He had often wondered what the aliens might think about his fascination with the rifle range, with that primal force that drove a man to kill, not for the joy of killing so much as to negate a danger, to meet force with a greater and more skillful force, cunning with more cunning. Had he, he wondered, given his alien friends concern in their assessment of the human character by his preoccupation with the rifle? For the understanding of an alien, how could one draw a line between the killing of other forms of life and the killing of one's own? Was there actually a differential that would stand up under logical examination between the sport of hunting and the sport of war? To an alien, perhaps, such a differentiation would be rather difficult, for in many cases the hunted animal would be more closely allied to the human hunter in its form and characteristics than would many of the aliens.

Was war an instinctive thing, for which each ordinary man was as much responsible as the policy makers and the so-called statesmen? It seemed impossible, and yet, deep in every man was the combative instinct, the aggressive urge, the strange sense of competition—all of which spelled conflict of one kind or another if carried to conclusion.

He put the rifle underneath his arm and walked over to the panel. Sticking from a slot in the bottom of it was a piece of tape.

He pulled it out and puzzled out the symbols. They were not reassuring. He had not done so well.

He had missed that first shot he had fired at the charging wolf-thing with the old man's face, and back there somewhere, in that dimension of unreality, it and its companion were snarling over the tangled, torn mass of ribboned flesh and broken bone that had been Enoch Wallace.

30

He went back through the gallery, with its gifts stacked there as other gifts, in regular human establishments, might be stacked away in dry and dusty attics.

The tape nagged at him, the little piece of tape which said that while he had made all his other shots, he had missed that first one back there on the hillock. It was not often that he missed. And his training had been for that very type of shooting—the you-never-know-what-will-happen-next, the totally unexpected, the kill-or-be-killed kind of shooting that thousands of expeditions into the target area had taught him. Perhaps, he consoled himself, he had not been as faithful in his practice lately as he should have been. Although there actually was no reason that he should be faithful, for the shooting was for recreation only and his carrying of the rifle on his daily walks was from force of habit only and for no other reason. He carried the rifle as another man might take along a cane or walking stick. At the time he had first done it, of course, it had been a different kind of rifle and a different day. It then was no unusual thing for a man to carry a gun while out on a walk. But today was different and he wondered, with an inner grin, how much talk his carrying a gun might have furnished the people who had seen him with it.

Near the end of the gallery he saw the black bulk of a trunk projecting from beneath the lower shelf, too big to fit comfortably beneath it, jammed against the wall, but with a foot or two of it still projecting out beyond the shelf.

He went on walking past it, then suddenly turned around. That trunk, he thought—that was the trunk which had belonged to the Hazer who had died upstairs. It was his legacy from that being whose stolen body would be brought back to its grave this evening.

He walked over to the shelving and leaned his rifle against the wall. Stooping, he pulled the trunk clear of its resting place.

Once before, prior to carrying it down the stairs and storing it here beneath the shelves, he had gone through its contents, but at the time, he recalled, he'd not been too interested. Now, suddenly, he felt an absorbing interest in it.

He lifted the lid carefully and tilted it back against the shelves.

Crouching above the open trunk, and without touching anything to start with, he tried to catalogue the upper layer of its contents.

There was a shimmering cloak, neatly folded, perhaps some sort of ceremonial cloak, although he could not know. And atop the cloak lay a tiny bottle that was a blaze of reflected light, as if someone had taken a large-sized diamond and hollowed it out to make a bottle of it. Beside the cloak lay a nest of balls, deep violet and dull, with no shine at all, looking for all the world like a bunch of table-tennis balls that someone had cemented together to make a globe. But that was not the way it was, Enoch remembered, for that other time he had been entranced by them and had picked them up, to find that they were not cemented, but could be freely moved about, although never outside the context of their shape. One ball could not be broken from the mass, no matter how hard one might try, but would move about, as if buoyed in a fluid, among all the other balls. One could move any, or all, of the balls, but the mass remained the same. A calculator of some sort, Enoch wondered, but that seemed only barely possible, for one ball was entirely like another, there was no way in which they could be identified. Or at least, no way to identify them by the human eye. Was it possible, he wondered, that identification might be possible to a Hazer's eye? And if a calculator, what kind of a calculator? Mathematical? Or ethical? Or philosophical? Although that was slightly foolish, for who had ever heard of a calculator for ethics or philosophy? Or, rather, what human had ever heard? More than likely it was not a calculator, but something else entirely. Perhaps a sort of game—a game of solitaire?

Given time, a man might finally get it figured out. But there was no time and no incentive at the moment to spend upon one particular item any great amount of time when there were hundreds of other items equally fantastic and incomprehensible. For while one puzzled over a single item, the edges of his mind would always wonder if he might not be spending time on the most insignificant of the entire lot.

He was a victim of museum fatigue, Enoch told himself, overwhelmed by the many pieces of the unknown scattered all about him.

He reached out a hand, not for the globe of balls, but for the shining bottle that lay atop the cloak. As he picked it up and brought it closer, he saw that there was a line of writing engraved upon the glass (or diamond?) of the bottle. Slowly he studied out the writing. There had been a time, long ago, when he had been able to read the Hazer language, if not fluently, at least well enough to get along. But he had not read it for some years now and he had lost a good deal of it and he stumbled haltingly from one symbol to another. Translated very freely, the inscription on the bottle read: *To be taken when the first symptoms occur.*

A bottle of medicine! To be taken when the first symptoms occur. The symptoms, perhaps, that had come so quickly and built up so rapidly that the owner of this bottle could make no move to reach it and so had died, falling from the sofa.

Almost reverently, he put the bottle back in its place atop the cloak, fitting it back into the faint impression it had made from lying there.

So different from us in so many ways, thought Enoch, and then in other little ways so like us that it is frightening. For that bottle and the inscription on its face was an exact parallel of the prescription bottle that could be compounded by any corner drugstore.

Beside the globe of balls was a box, and he reached out and lifted it. It was made of wood and had a rather simple clasp to hold it shut. He flipped back the lid and inside he saw the metallic sheen of the material the Hazers used as paper.

Carefully he lifted out the first sheet and saw that it was not a sheet, but a long strip of the material folded in accordion fashion. Underneath it were more strips, apparently of the same material.

There was writing on it, faint and faded, and Enoch held it close to read it.

To my —, — *friend:* (although it was not "friend." "Blood brother," perhaps, or "colleague." And the adjectives which preceded it were such as to escape his sense entirely.)

The writing was hard to read. It bore some resemblance to the formalized version of the language, but apparently bore the imprint of the writer's personality, expressed in curlicues and flourishes which obscured the form. Enoch worked his way slowly down the paper, missing much of what was there, but picking up the sense of much that had been written.

The writer had been on a visit to some other planet, or possibly just some other place. The name of the place or planet was one that Enoch did not recognize. While he had been there he had performed some sort of function (although exactly what it was was not entirely clear) which had to do with his approaching death.

Enoch, startled, went back over the phrase again. And while much of the rest of what was written was not clear, that part of it was. *My approaching death,* he had written, and there was no room for mistranslation. All three of the words were clear.

He urged that his good (friend?) do likewise. He said it was a comfort and made clear the road.

There was no further explanation, no further reference. Just the calm declaration that he had done something which he felt must be arranged about his death. As if he knew that death was near and was not only unafraid, but almost unconcerned.

The next passage (for there were no paragraphs) told about someone he had met and how they'd talked about a certain matter which made no sense at all to Enoch, who found himself lost in a terminology he did not recognize.

And then: *I am most concerned about the mediocrity* (incompetence? inability? weakness?) *of the recent custodian of* (and then that cryptic symbol which could be translated, roughly, as the Talisman.) *For* (a word, which from the context, seemed to mean a great length of time), *ever since the death of the last custodian, the Talisman has been but poorly served. It has been, in all reality,* (another long time term), *since a true* (sensitive?) *has been found to carry out its purpose. Many have been tested and none has qualified, and for the lack of such a one the galaxy has lost its close identification with the ruling principle of life. We here at the* (temple? sanctuary?) *all are greatly concerned that without a proper linkage between the people and* (several words that were not decipherable) *the galaxy will go down in chaos* (and another line that he could not puzzle out).

The next sentence introduced a new subject—the plans that were going forward for some cultural festival which concerned a concept that, to Enoch, was hazy at the best.

Enoch slowly folded up the letter and put it back into the box. He felt a faint uneasiness in reading what he had, as if he'd pried into a friendship that he had no right to know. *We here at the temple,* the letter had said. Perhaps the writer had been one of the Hazer mystics, writing to his old friend, the philosopher. And the other letters, quite possibly, were from that same mystic—letters that the dead old Hazer had valued so highly that he took them along with him when he went traveling.

A slight breeze seemed to be blowing across Enoch's shoulders;

oldness to

thing stir-

wn. Here

ht Enoch.

nt he had

ad known

ad spoken

e capacity

th.

and death

out, put

sitories in

be, that

destiny.

personal

ce might

the uni-

ght tie in

time and

universe

n contact

ose who

s to tell.

one who

and time

about the

and that

or many

years its power and gl

custodian to provide

the force. And all th

failure had eaten awa

Whatever might be li

last few years; it had

most aliens would ad

aliens probably did no

Enoch closed the be

day, he thought, wh

when the pressure o

he could dull the gui

and conscientious tra

felt certain, he migh

guing race. He migh

their humanity—not

sense of being a me

the sense that certai

concepts even as the

underlay the human

He reached up to

hesitated.

Some day, he had

It was a state of mi

of mind made possib

here there were end

were days to come.

shape and reason an

long, almost never

all over now. Time

focus. Should he le

to come would end

He pushed back t

Reaching in, he lift

him. He'd take it u

not actually a breeze, but a strange motion and a coldness to the air.

He glanced back into the gallery and there was nothing stirring, nothing to be seen.

The wind had quit its blowing, if it had ever blown. Here one moment, gone the next. Like a passing ghost, thought Enoch.

Did the Hazer have a ghost?

The people back on Vega XXI had known the moment he had died and all the circumstances of his death. They had known again about the body disappearing. And the letter had spoken calmly, much more calmly than would have been in the capacity of most humans, about the writer's near approach to death.

Was it possible that the Hazers knew more of life and death than had ever been spelled out? Or had it been spelled out, put down in black and white, in some depository or depositories in the galaxy?

Was the answer there? he wondered.

Squatting there, he thought that perhaps it might be, that someone already knew what life was for and what its destiny. There was a comfort in the thought, a strange sort of personal comfort in being able to believe that some intelligence might have solved the riddle of that mysterious equation of the universe. And how, perhaps, that mysterious equation might tie in with the spiritual force that was idealistic brother to time and space and all those other elemental factors that held the universe together.

He tried to imagine what one might feel if he were in contact with the force, and could not. He wondered if even those who might have been in contact with it could find the words to tell. It might, he thought, be impossible. For how could one who had been in intimate contact all his life with space and time tell what either of these meant to him or how they felt?

Ulysses, he thought, had not told him all the truth about the Talisman. He had told him that it had disappeared and that the galaxy was without it, but he had not told him that for many years its power and glory had been dimmed by the failure of its custodian to provide a proper linkage between the people and the force. And all that time the corrosion occasioned by that failure had eaten away at the bonds of the galactic cofraternity. Whatever might be happening now had not happened in the last few years; it had been building up for a longer time than most aliens would admit. Although, come to think of it, most aliens probably did not know.

Enoch closed the box lid and put it back into the trunk. Some day, he thought, when he was in the proper frame of mind, when the pressure of events made him less emotional, when he could dull the guilt of prying, he would achieve a scholarly and conscientious translation of those letters. For in them, he felt certain, he might find further understanding of that intriguing race. He might, he thought, then be better able to gauge *their* humanity—not humanity in the common and accepted sense of being a member of the human race of Earth, but in the sense that certain rules of conduct must underlie all racial concepts even as the thing called humanity in its narrow sense underlay the human concept.

He reached up to close the lid of the trunk and then he hesitated.

Some day, he had said. And there might not be a some day. It was a state of mind to be always thinking *some day,* a state of mind made possible by the conditions inside this station. For here there were endless days to come, forever and forever there were days to come. A man's concept of time was twisted out of shape and reason and he could look ahead complacently down a long, almost never ending, avenue of time. But that might be all over now. Time might suddenly snap back into its rightful focus. Should he leave this station, the long procession of days to come would end.

He pushed back the lid again until it rested against the shelves. Reaching in, he lifted out the box and set it on the floor beside him. He'd take it upstairs, he told himself, and put it with the other stuff that he must be prepared immediately to take along with him if he should leave the station.

If? he asked himself. Was there a question any longer? Had he, somehow, made that hard decision? Had it crept upon him unaware, so that he now was committed to it?

And if he had actually arrived at that decision, then he must, also, have arrived at the other one. If he left the station, then he could no longer be in a position to appear before Galactic Central to plead that Earth be cured of war.

You are the representative of the Earth, Ulysses had told him. You are the only one who can represent the Earth. But could he, in reality, represent the Earth? Was he any longer a true representative of the human race? He was a nineteenth-century man and how could he, being that, represent the twentieth? How much, he wondered, does the human character change with each generation? And not only was he of the nineteenth century, but he had, as well, lived for almost a hundred years under a separate and a special circumstance.

He knelt there, regarding himself with awe, and a little pity, too, wondering what he was, if he were even human, if, unknown to himself, he had absorbed so much of the mingled alien viewpoint to which he had been subjected that he had become some strange sort of hybrid, a queer kind of galactic half-breed.

Slowly he pulled the lid down and pushed it tight. Then he shoved the trunk back underneath the shelves.

He tucked the box of letters underneath his arm and rose, picking up his rifle, and headed for the stairs.

31

He found some empty cartons stacked in the kitchen corner, boxes that Winslowe had used to bring out from town the supplies that he had ordered, and began to pack.

The journals, stacked neatly in order, filled one large box and a part of another. He took a stack of old newspapers and carefully wrapped the twelve diamond bottles off the mantel and packed them in another box, thickly padded, to guard against their breakage. Out of the cabinet he got the Vegan music box and wrapped it as carefully. He pulled out of another cabinet the alien literature that he had and piled it in the fourth box. He went through his desk, but there wasn't too much there, only odds and ends tucked here and there throughout the drawers. He found his chart and, crumpling it, threw it in the wastebasket that stood beside his desk.

The already filled boxes he carried across the room and stacked beside the door for easy reaching. Lewis would have a truck, but once he let him know he needed it, it still might take a while for it to arrive. But if he had the important stuff all packed, he told himself, he could get it out himself and have it waiting for the truck.

The important stuff, he thought. Who could judge importance? The journals and the alien literature, those first of all, of course. But the rest of it? Which of the rest of it? It was all important; every item should be taken. And that might be possible. Given time and with no extra complications, it might be possible to haul it all away, all that was in this room and stored down in the basement. It all was his and he had a right to it, for it had been given him. But that did not mean, he knew, that Galactic Central might not object most strenuously to his taking any of it.

And if that should happen, it was vital that he should be able to get away with those most important items. Perhaps he should go down into the basement and lug up those tagged articles of which he knew the purpose. It probably would be better to take material about which something might be known than a lot of stuff about which there was nothing known.

He stood undecided, looking all about the room. There were all the items on the coffee table and those should be taken, too, including the little flashing pyramid of globes that Lucy had set to working.

He saw that the Pet once again had crawled off the table and fallen on the floor. He stooped and picked it up and held it in his hands. It had grown an extra knob or two since the last time he had looked at it and it was now a faint and delicate pink, whereas the last time he had noticed it had been a cobalt blue.

He probably was wrong, he told himself, in calling it the Pet. It might not be alive. But if it were, it was a sort of life he could not even guess at. It was not metallic and it was not stone, but very close to both. A file made no impression on it and he'd been tempted a time or two to whack it with a hammer to see what that might do, although he was willing to bet it would have no effect at all. It grew slowly, and it moved, but there was no way of knowing how it moved. But leave it and come back and it would have moved—a little, not too much. It knew it was being watched and it would not move while watched. It did not eat so far as he could see and it seemed to have no wastes. It changed colors, but entirely without season and with no visible reason for the change.

A being from somewhere in the direction of Sagittarius had given it to him just a year or two ago, and the creature, Enoch recalled, had been something for the books. He probably wasn't actually a walking plant, but that was what he'd looked like—a rather spindly plant that had been shorted on good water and cheated on good soil, but which had sprouted a crop of dime-store bangles that rang like a thousand silver bells when he made any sort of motion.

Enoch remembered that he had tried to ask the being what the gift might be, but the walking plant had simply clashed its bangles and filled the place with ringing sound and didn't try to answer.

So he had put the gift on one end of the desk and hours later, after the being was long gone, he found that it had moved to the other end of the desk. But it had seemed too crazy to think that a thing like that could move, so he finally convinced himself that he was mistaken as to where he'd put it. It was not until days later that he was able to convince himself it moved.

He'd have to take it when he left and Lucy's pyramid and the cube that showed you pictures of other worlds when you looked inside of it and a great deal of other stuff.

He stood with the Pet held in his hand and now, for the first time, he wondered at why he might be packing.

He was acting as if he'd decided he would leave the station, as if he'd chosen Earth as against the galaxy. But when and how, he wondered, had he decided it? Decision should be based on weighing and on measuring and he had weighed and measured nothing. He had not posed the advantages and the disadvantages and tried to strike a balance. He had not thought it out. Somehow, somewhere, it had sneaked up on him—this decision which had seemed impossible, but now had been reached so easily.

Was it, he wondered, that he had absorbed, unconsciously, such an odd mixture of alien thought and ethics that he had evolved, unknown to himself, a new way in which to think, perhaps some subconscious way of thought that had lain inoperative until now, when it had been needed.

There was a box or two out in the shed and he'd go and get them and finish up the packing of what he'd pick out here. Then he'd go down into the basement and start lugging up the stuff that he had tagged. He glanced toward the window and realized, with some surprise, that he would have to hurry, for the sun was close to setting. It would be evening soon.

He remembered that he'd forgotten lunch, but he had no time to eat. He could get something later.

He turned to put the Pet back on the table and as he did a faint sound caught his ear and froze him where he stood.

It was the slight chuckle of a materializer operating and he could not mistake it. He had heard the sound too often to be able to mistake it.

And it must be, he knew, the official materializer, for no one could have traveled on the other without the sending of a message.

Ulysses, he thought. Ulysses coming back again. Or perhaps some other member of Galactic Central. For if Ulysses had been coming, he would have sent a message.

He took a quick step forward so he could see the corner where the materializer stood and a dark and slender figure was stepping out from the target circle.

"Ulysses!" Enoch cried, but even as he spoke he realized it was not Ulysses.

For an instant he had the impression of a top hat, of white tie and tails, of a jauntiness, and then he saw that the creature was a rat that walked erect, with sleek, dark fur covering its body and a sharp, axlike rodent face. For an instant, as it turned its head toward him, he caught the red glitter of its eyes. Then it turned back toward the corner and he saw that its hand was lifted and was pulling out of a harnessed holster hung about its middle something that glinted with a metallic shimmer even in the shadow.

There was something very wrong about it. The creature should have greeted him. It should have said hello and come out to meet him. But instead it had thrown him that one red-eyed glance and then turned back to the corner.

The metallic object came out of the holster and it could only

be a gun, or at least some sort of weapon that one might think
of as a gun.

And was this the way, thought Enoch, that they would close
the station? One quick shot, without a word, and the station
keeper dead upon the floor. With someone other than Ulysses,
because Ulysses could not be trusted to kill a long-time friend.

The rifle was lying across the desk top and there wasn't any
time.

But the ratlike creature was not turning toward the room. It
still was facing toward the corner and its hand was coming up,
with the weapon glinting in it.

An alarm twanged within Enoch's brain and he swung his
arm and yelled, hurling the Pet toward the creature in the corner,
the yell jerked out of him involuntarily from the bottom of his
lungs.

For the creature, he realized, had not been intent on the killing of the keeper, but the disruption of the station. The only
thing there was to aim at in the corner was the control complex,
the nerve center of the station's operation. And if that should
be knocked out, the station would be dead. To set it in operation
once again it would be necessary to send a crew of technicians
out in a spaceship from the nearest station—a trip that would
require many years to make.

At Enoch's yell, the creature jerked around, dropping toward
a crouch, and the flying Pet, tumbling end for end, caught it
in the belly and drove it back against the wall.

Enoch charged, arms outspread to grapple with the creature.
The gun flew from the creature's hand and pinwheeled across
the floor. Then Enoch was upon the alien and even as he closed
with it, his nostrils were assailed by its body stench—a sickening
wave of nastiness.

He wrapped his arms about it and heaved, and it was not as
heavy as he had thought it might be. His powerful wrench jerked
it from the corner and swung it around and sent it skidding
out across the floor.

It crashed against a chair and came to a stop and then like a steel coil it rose off the floor and pounced for the gun.

Enoch took two great strides and had it by the neck, lifting it and shaking it so savagely that the recovered gun flew from its hand again and the bag it carried on a thong across its shoulder pounded like a vibrating trip hammer against its hairy ribs.

The stench was thick, so thick that one could almost see it, and Enoch gagged on it as he shook the creature. And suddenly it was worse, much worse, like a fire raging in one's throat and a hammer in one's head. It was like a physical blow that hit one in the belly and shoved against the chest. Enoch let go his hold upon the creature and staggered back, doubled up and retching. He lifted his hands to his face and tried to push the stench away, to clear his nostrils and his mouth, to rub it from his eyes.

Through a haze he saw the creature rise and, snatching up the gun, rush toward the door. He did not hear the phrase that the creature spoke, but the door came open and the creature spurted forward and was gone. And the door slammed shut again.

32

Enoch wobbled across the room to the desk and caught at it for support. The stench was diminishing and his head was clearing and he scarcely could believe that it all had happened. For it was incredible that a thing like this should happen. The creature had traveled on the official materializer, and no one but a member of Galactic Central could travel by that route. And no member of Galactic Central, he was convinced, would have acted as the ratlike creature had. Likewise, the creature had known the phrase that would operate the door. No one but himself and Galactic Central would have known that phrase.

He reached out and picked up his rifle and hefted it in his fist.

It was all right, he thought. There was nothing harmed. Except that there was an alien loose upon the Earth and that was something that could not be allowed. The Earth was barred to aliens. As a planet which had not been recognized by the galactic cofraternity, it was off-limit territory.

He stood with the rifle in his hand and knew what he must do—he must get that alien back, he must get it off the Earth.

He spoke the phrase aloud and strode toward the door and out and around the corner of the house.

The alien was running across the field and had almost reached the line of woods.

Enoch ran desperately, but before he was halfway down the field, the ratlike quarry had plunged into the woods and disappeared.

The woods was beginning to darken. The slanting rays of light from the setting sun still lighted the upper canopy of the foliage, but on the forest floor the shadows had begun to gather.

As he ran into the fringe of the woods, Enoch caught a glimpse of the creature angling down a small ravine and plunging up the other slope, racing through a heavy cover of ferns that reached almost to its middle.

If it kept on in that direction, Enoch told himself, it might work out all right, for the slope beyond the ravine ended in a clump of rocks that lay above an outthrust point that ended in a cliff, with each side curving in, so that the point and its mass of boulders lay isolated, a place hung out in space. It might be a little rough to dig the alien from the rocks if it took refuge there, but at least it would be trapped and could not get away. Although, Enoch reminded himself, he could waste no time, for the sun was setting and it would soon be dark.

Enoch angled slightly westward to go around the head of the small ravine, keeping an eye on the fleeing alien. The creature kept on up the slope and Enoch, observing this, put on an extra burst of speed. For now he had the alien trapped. In its fleeing, it had gone past the point of no return. It could no longer turn around and retreat back from the point. Soon it would reach the cliff edge and then there'd be nothing it could do but hole up in the patch of boulders.

Running hard, Enoch crossed the area covered by the ferns and came out on the sharper slope some hundred yards or so below the boulder clump. Here the cover was not so dense. There was a scant covering of spotty underbrush and a scattering of trees. The soft loam of the forest floor gave way to a footing of shattered rock which through the years had been chipped off the boulders by the winters' frost, rolling down the slope. They lay there now, covered with thick moss, a treacherous place to walk.

As he ran, Enoch swept the boulders with a glance, but there was no sign of the alien. Then, out of the corner of his vision, he saw the motion, and threw himself forward to the ground behind a patch of hazel brush, and through the network of the bushes he saw the alien outlined against the sky, its head pivoting back and forth to sweep the slope below, the weapon half lifted and set for instant use.

Enoch lay frozen, with his outstretched hand gripping the rifle. There was a slash of pain across one set of knuckles and he knew that he had skinned them on the rock as he had dived for cover.

The alien dropped from sight behind the boulders and Enoch slowly pulled the rifle back to where he would be able to handle it should a shot present itself.

Although, he wondered, would he dare to fire? Would he dare to kill an alien?

The alien could have killed him back there at the station, when he had been knocked silly by the dreadful stench. But it had not killed him; it had fled instead. Was it, he wondered, that the creature had been so badly frightened that all that it could think of had been to get away? Or had it, perhaps, been as reluctant to kill a station keeper as he himself was to kill an alien?

He searched the rocks above him and there was no motion and not a thing to see. He must move up that slope, and quickly, he told himself, for time would work against him and to the advantage of the alien. Darkness could not be more than thirty minutes off and before dark had fallen this issue must be settled. If the alien got away, there'd be little chance to find it.

And why, asked a second self, standing to one side, should you worry about alien complications? For are you yourself not prepared to inform the Earth that there are alien peoples in the galaxy and to hand to Earth, unauthorized, as much of that alien lore and learning as may be within your power? Why should you have stopped this alien from the wrecking of the station, insuring its isolation for many years—for if that had been done, then you'd have been free to do as you might wish with all that is within the station? It would have worked to your advantage to have allowed events to run their course.

But I couldn't, Enoch cried inside himself. *Don't you see I couldn't? Don't you understand?*

A rustle in the bushes to his left brought him around with the rifle up and ready.

And there was Lucy Fisher, not more than twenty feet away.

"Get out of here!" he shouted, forgetting that she could not hear him.

But she did not seem to notice. She motioned to the left and made a sweeping motion with her hand and pointed toward the boulders.

Go away, he said underneath his breath. *Go away from here.*

And made rejection motions to indicate that she should go back, that this was no place for her.

She shook her head and sprang away, in a running crouch, moving further to the left and up the slope.

Enoch scrambled to his feet, lunging after her, and as he did the air behind him made a frying sound and there was the sharp bite of ozone in the air.

He hit the ground, instinctively, and farther down the slope he saw a square yard of ground that boiled and steamed, with the ground cover swept away by a fierce heat and the very soil and rock turned into a simmering pudding.

A laser, Enoch thought. The alien's weapon was a laser, packing a terrific punch in a narrow beam of light.

He gathered himself together and made a short rush up the hillside, throwing himself prone behind a twisted birch clump.

The air made the frying sound again and there was an instant's blast of heat and the ozone once again. Over on the reverse slope a patch of ground was steaming. Ash floated down and settled on Enoch's arms. He flashed a quick glance upward and saw that the top half of the birch clump was gone, sheared off by the laser and reduced to ash. Tiny coils of smoke rose lazily from the severed stumps.

No matter what it may have done, or failed to do, back there at the station, the alien now meant business. It knew that it was cornered and it was playing vicious.

Enoch huddled against the ground and worried about Lucy. He hoped that she was safe. The little fool should have stayed out of it. This was no place for her. She shouldn't even have been out in the woods at this time of day. She'd have old Hank out looking for her again, thinking she was kidnaped. He wondered what the hell had gotten into her.

The dusk was deepening. Only the far peak of the treetops caught the last rays of the sun. A coolness came stealing up the ravine from the valley far below and there was a damp, lush smell that came out of the ground. From some hidden hollow a whippoorwill called out mournfully.

Enoch darted out from behind the birch clump and rushed up the slope. He reached the fallen log he'd picked as a barricade and threw himself behind it. There was no sign of the alien and there was not another shot from the laser gun.

Enoch studied the ground ahead. Two more rushes, one to that small pile of rock and the next to the edge of the boulder area itself, and he'd be on top of the hiding alien. And once he got there, he wondered, what was he to do.

Go in and rout the alien out, of course.

There was no plan that could be made, no tactics that could be laid out in advance. Once he got to the edge of the boulders, he must play it all by ear, taking advantage of any break that might present itself. He was at a disadvantage in that he must not kill the alien, but must capture it instead and drag it back, kicking and screaming, if need be, to the safety of the station.

Perhaps, here in the open air, it could not use its stench defense as effectively as it had in the confines of the station, and that, he thought, might make it easier. He examined the clump of boulders from one edge to the other and there was nothing that might help him to locate the alien.

Slowly he began to snake around, getting ready for the next rush up the slope, moving carefully so that no sound would betray him.

Out of the tail of his eye he caught the moving shadow that came flowing up the slope. Swiftly he sat up, swinging the rifle. But before he could bring the muzzle round, the shadow was upon him, bearing him back, flat upon the ground, with one great splay-fingered hand clamped upon his mouth.

"Ulysses!" Enoch gurgled, but the fearsome shape only hissed at him in a warning sound.

Slowly the weight shifted off him and the hand slid from his mouth.

Ulysses gestured toward the boulder pile and Enoch nodded.

Ulysses crept closer and lowered his head toward Enoch's. He whispered with his mouth inches from the Earthman's ear: "The Talisman! He has the Talisman!"

"The Talisman!" Enoch cried aloud, trying to strangle off the cry even as he made it, remembering that he should make no sound to let the watcher up above know where they might be.

From the ridge above a loose stone rattled as it was dislodged and began to roll, bouncing down the slope. Enoch hunkered closer to the ground behind the fallen log.

"Down!" he shouted to Ulysses. "Down! He has a gun."

But Ulysses's hand gripped him by the shoulder.

"Enoch!" he cried. "Enoch, look!"

Enoch jerked himself erect and atop the pile of rock, dark against the skyline, were two grappling figures.

"Lucy!" he shouted.

For one of them was Lucy and the other was the alien.

She sneaked up on him, he thought. The damn' little fool, she sneaked up on him! While the alien had been distracted with watching the slope, she had slipped up close and then had tackled him. She had a club of some sort in her hand, an old dead branch, perhaps, and it was raised above her head, ready for a stroke, but the alien had a grip upon her arm and she could not strike.

"Shoot," said Ulysses, in a flat, dead voice.

Enoch raised the rifle and had trouble with the sights because of the deepening darkness. And they were so close together! They were too close together.

"Shoot!" yelled Ulysses.

"I can't," sobbed Enoch. "It's too dark to shoot."

"You have to shoot," Ulysses said, his voice tense and hard. "You have to take the chance."

Enoch raised the rifle once again and the sights seemed clearer now and he knew the trouble was not so much the darkness as that shot which he had missed back there in the world of the honking thing that had strode its world on stilts. If he had missed then, he could as well miss now.

The bead came to rest upon the head of the ratlike creature, and then the head bobbed away, but was bobbing back again.

"Shoot!" Ulysses yelled.

Enoch squeezed the trigger and the rifle coughed and up atop the rocks the creature stood for a second with only half a head and with tattered gouts of flesh flying briefly like dark insects zooming against the half-light of the western sky.

Enoch dropped the gun and sprawled upon the earth, clawing his fingers into the thin and mossy soil, sick with the thought of what could have happened, weak with the thankfulness that it had not happened, that the years on that fantastic rifle range had at last paid off.

How strange it is, he thought, how so many senseless things shape our destiny. For the rifle range had been a senseless thing, as senseless as a billiard table or a game of cards—designed for one thing only, to please the keeper of the station. And yet the hours he'd spent there had shaped toward this hour and end, to this single instant on this restricted slope of ground.

The sickness drained away into the earth beneath him and a peace came stealing in upon him—the peace of trees and woodland soil and the first faint hush of nightfall. As if the sky and stars and very space itself had leaned close above him and was whispering his essential oneness with them. And it seemed for a moment that he had grasped the edge of some great truth and with this truth had come a comfort and a greatness he'd never known before.

"Enoch," Ulysses whispered. "Enoch, my brother . . ."

There was something like a hidden sob in the alien's voice and he had never, until this moment, called the Earthman brother.

Enoch pulled himself to his knees and up on the pile of tumbled boulders was a soft and wondrous light, a soft and gentle light, as if a giant firefly had turned on its lamp and had not turned it off, but had left it burning.

The light was moving down across the rocks toward them and he could see Lucy moving with the light, as if she were walking toward them with a lantern in her hand.

Ulysses's hand reached out of the darkness and closed hard on Enoch's arm.

"Do you see?" he asked.

"Yes, I see. What is . . ."

"It is the Talisman," Ulysses said, enraptured, his breath rasping in his throat. "And she is our new custodian. The one we've hunted through the years."

33

You did not become accustomed to it, Enoch told himself as they tramped up through the woods. There was not a moment you were not aware of it. It was something that you wanted to hug close against yourself and hold it there forever, and even when it was gone from you, you'd probably not forget it, ever.

It was something that was past all description—a mother's love, a father's pride, the adoration of a sweetheart, the closeness of a comrade, it was all of these and more. It made the farthest distance near and turned the complex simple and it swept away all fear and sorrow, for all of there being a certain feeling of deep sorrow in it, as if one might feel that never in his lifetime would he know an instant like this, and that in another instant he would lose it and never would be able to hunt it out again. But that was not the way it was, for this ascendant instant kept going on and on.

Lucy walked between them and she held the bag that contained the Talisman close against her breast, with her two arms clasped about it, and Enoch, looking at her, in the soft glow of its light, could not help but think of a little girl carrying her beloved pussy cat.

"Never for a century," said Ulysses, "perhaps for many centuries, perhaps never, has it glowed so well. I myself cannot remember when it was like this. It is wonderful, is it not?"

"Yes," said Enoch. "It is wonderful."

"Now we shall be one again," Ulysses said. "Now we shall feel again. Now we shall be a people instead of many people."

"But the creature that had it . . ."

"A clever one," Ulysses said. "He was holding it for ransom."

"It had been stolen, then."

"We do not know all the circumstances," Ulysses told him. "We will find out, of course."

They tramped on in silence through the woods and far in the east one could see, through the treetops, the first flush in the sky that foretold the rising moon.

"There is something," Enoch said.

"Ask me," said Ulysses.

"How could that creature back there carry it and not feel—feel no part of it? For if he could have, he would not have stolen it."

"There is only one in many billions," Ulysses said, "who can —how do you say it?—tune in on it, perhaps. To you and I it would be nothing. It would not respond to us. We could hold it in our hands forever and there would nothing happen. But let that one in many billions lay a finger on it and it becomes alive. There is a certain rapport, a sensitivity—I don't know how to say it—that forms a bridge between this strange machine and the cosmic spiritual force. It is not the machine, itself, you understand, that reaches out and taps the spiritual force. It is the living creature's mind, aided by the mechanism, that brings the force to us."

A machine, a mechanism, no more than a tool—technological brother to the hoe, the wrench, the hammer—and yet as far a cry from these as the human brain was from that first amino acid which had come into being on this planet when the Earth was very young. One was tempted, Enoch thought, to say that this was as far as a tool could go, that it was the ultimate in the ingenuity possessed by any brain. But that would be a dangerous way of thinking, for perhaps there was no limit, there might, quite likely, be no such condition as the ultimate; there might be no time when any creature or any group of creatures could stop at any certain point and say, this is as far as we can go, there is no use of trying to go farther. For each new development produced, as side effects, so many other possibilities, so many other roads to travel, that with each step one took down any given road there were more paths to follow. There'd never be an end, he thought—no end to anything.

They reached the edge of the field and headed up across it toward the station. From its upper edge came the sound of running feet.

"Enoch!" a voice shouted out of the darkness. "Enoch, is that you?"

Enoch recognized the voice.

"Yes, Winslowe. What is wrong?"

The mailman burst out of the darkness and stopped, panting with his running, at the edge of light.

"Enoch, they are coming! A couple of carloads of them. But I put a crimp in them. Where the road turns off into your lane— that narrow place, you know. I dumped two pounds of roofing nails along the ruts. That'll hold them for a while."

"Roofing nails?" Ulysses asked.

"It's a mob," Enoch told him. "They are after me. The nails . . ."

"Oh, I see," Ulysses said. "The deflation of the tires."

Winslowe took a slow step closer, his gaze riveted on the glow of the shielded Talisman.

"That's Lucy Fisher, ain't it?"

"Of course it is," said Enoch.

"Her old man came roaring into town just a while ago and said she was gone again. Up until then everything had quieted down and it was all right. But old Hank, he got them stirred up again. So I went down to the hardware store and got them roofing nails and I beat them here."

"This mob?" Ulysses asked. "I don't . . ."

Winslowe interrupted him, gasping in his eagerness to tell

all his information. "That ginseng man is up there, waiting at the house for you. He has a panel truck."

"That," said Enoch, "would be Lewis with the Hazer's body."

"He is some upset," said Winslowe. "He said you were expecting him."

"Perhaps," suggested Ulysses, "we shouldn't just be standing here. It seems to my poor intellect that many things, indeed, may be coming to a crisis."

"Say," the mailman yelled, "what is going on here? What is that thing Lucy has and who's this fellow with you?"

"Later," Enoch told him. "I'll tell you later. There's no time to tell you now."

"But, Enoch, there's the mob."

"I'll deal with them," said Enoch grimly, "when I have to deal with them. Right now there's something more important."

They ran up the slope, the four of them, dodging through the waist-high clumps of weeds. Ahead of them the station reared dark and angular against the evening sky.

"They're down there at the turnoff," Winslowe gasped, wheezing with his running. "That flash of light down the ridge. That was the headlights of a car."

They reached the edge of the yard and ran toward the house. The black bulk of the panel truck glimmered in the glow cast by the Talisman. A figure detached itself from the shadow of the truck and hurried out toward them.

"Is that you, Wallace?"

"Yes," said Enoch. "I'm sorry that I wasn't here."

"I was a bit upset," said Lewis, "when I didn't find you waiting."

"Something unforeseen," said Enoch. "Something that must be taken care of."

"The body of the honored one?" Ulysses asked. "It is in the truck?"

Lewis nodded. "I am happy that we can restore it."

"We'll have to carry him down to the orchard," Enoch said. "You can't get a car in there."

"The other time," Ulysses said, "you were the one who carried him."

Enoch nodded.

"My friend," the alien said, "I wonder if on this occasion I could be allowed the honor."

"Why, yes, of course," said Enoch. "He would like it that way."

And the words came to his tongue, but he choked them back, for it would not have done to say them—the words of thanks for lifting from him the necessity of complete recompense, for the gesture which released him from the utter letter of the law.

At his elbow, Winslowe said: "They are coming. I can hear them down the road."

He was right.

From down the road came the soft sound of footsteps padding in the dust, not hurrying, with no need to hurry, the insulting and deliberate treading of a monster so certain of its prey that it need not hurry.

Enoch swung around and half lifted his rifle, training it toward the padding that came out of the dark.

Behind him, Ulysses spoke softly: "Perhaps it would be most proper to bear him to the grave in the full glory and unshielded light of our restored Talisman."

"She can't hear you," Enoch said. "You must remember she is deaf. You will have to show her."

But even as he said it, a blaze leaped out that was blinding in its brightness.

With a strangled cry Enoch half turned back to face the little group that stood beside the truck, and the bag that had enclosed the Talisman, he saw, lay at Lucy's feet and she held the glowing brightness high and proudly so that it spread its light across the yard and the ancient house, and some of it as well spilled out into the field.

There was a quietness. As if the entire world had caught its breath and stood attentive and in awe, waiting for a sound that did not come, that would never come but would always be expected.

And with the quietness came an abiding sense of peace that seemed to seep into the very fiber of one's being. It was no synthetic thing—not as if someone had invoked a peace and peace then was allowed to exist by suffrance. It was a present and an actual peace, the peace of mind that came with the calmness of a sunset after a long, hot day, or the sparkling, ghost-like shimmer of a springtime dawn. You felt it inside of you and all about you, and there was the feeling that it was not only here but that the peace extended on and out in all directions, to the farthest reaches of infinity, and that it had a depth which would enable it to endure until the final gasp of all eternity.

Slowly, remembering, Enoch turned back to face the field and the men were there, at the edge of the light cast by the Talisman, a gray, huddled group, like a pack of chastened wolves that slunk at the faint periphery of a campfire's light.

And as he watched, they melted back—back into the deeper dark from which they had padded in the dust track of the road.

Except for one who turned and bolted, plunging down the hill in the darkness toward the woods, howling in maddened terror like a frightened dog.

"There goes Hank," said Winslowe. "That is Hank running down the hill."

"I am sorry that we frightened him," said Enoch soberly. "No man should be afraid of this."

"It is himself that he is frightened of," the mailman said. "He lives with a terror in him."

And that was true, thought Enoch. That was the way with Man; it had always been that way. He had carried terror with him. And the thing he was afraid of had always been himself.

34

The grave was filled and mounded and the five of them stood for a moment more, listening to the restless wind that stirred in the moon-drenched apple orchard, while from far away, down in the hollows above the river valley, the whippoorwills talked back and forth through the silver night.

In the moonlight Enoch tried to read the graven line upon the rough-hewn tombstone, but there was not light enough. Although there was no need to read it; it was in his mind:

Here lies one from a distant star, but the soil is not alien to him, for in death he belongs to the universe.

When you wrote that, the Hazer diplomat had told him, just the night before, you wrote as one of us. And he had not said so, but the Vegan had been wrong. For it was not a Vegan sentiment alone; it was human, too.

The words were chiseled awkwardly and there was a mistake or two in spelling, for the Hazer language was not an easy one to master. The stone was softer than the marble or the granite most commonly used for gravestones and the lettering would not last. In a few more years the weathering of sun and rain and frost would blur the characters, and in some years after that they would be entirely gone, with no more than the roughness of the stone remaining to show that words had once been written there. But it did not matter, Enoch thought, for the words were graven on more than stone alone.

He looked across the grave at Lucy. The Talisman was in its bag once more and the glow was softer. She still held it clasped tight against herself and her face was still exalted and unnoticing —as if she no longer lived in the present world, but had entered into some other place, some other far dimension where she dwelled alone and was forgetful of all past.

"Do you think," Ulysses asked, "that she will go with us? Do you think that we can have her? Will the Earth . . ."

"The Earth," said Enoch, "has not a thing to say. We Earth people are free agents. It is up to her."

"You think that she will go?"

"I think so," Enoch said. "I think maybe this has been the moment she had sought for all her life. I wonder if she might not have sensed it, even with no Talisman."

For she always had been in touch with something outside of human ken. She had something in her no other human had. You sensed it, but you could not name it, for there was no name for this thing she had. And she had fumbled with it, trying to use it, not knowing how to use it, charming off the warts and healing poor hurt butterflies and only God knew what other acts that she performed unseen.

"Her parent?" Ulysses asked. "The howling one that ran away from us?"

"I'll handle him," said Lewis. "I'll have a talk with him. I know him fairly well."

"You want her to go back with you to Galactic Central?" Enoch asked.

"If she will," Ulysses said. "Central must be told at once."

"And from there throughout the galaxy?"

"Yes," Ulysses said. "We need her very badly."

"Could we, I wonder, borrow her for a day or two."

"Borrow her?"

"Yes," said Enoch. "For we need her, too. We need her worst of all."

"Of course," Ulysses said. "But I don't . . ."

"Lewis," Enoch asked, "do you think our government—the Secretary of State, perhaps—might be persuaded to appoint one Lucy Fisher as a member of our peace conference delegation?"

Lewis stammered, made a full stop, then began again: "I think it could possibly be managed."

"Can you imagine," Enoch asked, "the impact of this girl and the Talisman at the conference table?"

"I think I can," said Lewis. "But the Secretary undoubtedly would want to talk with you before he arrived at his decision."

Enoch half turned toward Ulysses, but he did not need to phrase his question.

"By all means," Ulysses said to Lewis. "Let me know and I'll sit in on the meeting. And you might tell the good Secretary, too, that it would not be a bad idea to begin the formation of a world committee."

"A world committee?"

"To arrange," Ulysses said, "for the Earth becoming one of us. We cannot accept a custodian, can we, from an outside planet?"

35

In the moonlight the tumbled boulder pile gleamed whitely, like the skeleton of some prehistoric beast. For here, near the edge of the cliff that towered above the river, the heavy trees thinned out and the rocky point stood open to the sky.

Enoch stood beside one of the massive boulders and gazed down at the huddled figure that lay among the rocks. Poor, tattered bungler, he thought, dead so far from home and, so far as he, himself, must be concerned, to so little purpose.

Although perhaps neither poor nor tattered, for in that brain, now broken and spattered beyond recovery, must surely have lain a scheme of greatness—the kind of scheme that the brain of an earthly Alexander or Xerxes or Napoleon may have held, a dream of some great power, cynically conceived, to be attained and held at whatever cost, the dimensions of it so grandiose that it shoved aside and canceled out all moral considerations.

He tried momentarily to imagine what the scheme might be, but knew, even as he tested his imagination, how foolish it was to try, for there would be factors, he was sure, that he would not recognize and considerations that might lie beyond his understanding.

But however that might be, something had gone wrong, for in the plan itself Earth could have had no place other than as a hideout which could be used if trouble struck. This creature's lying here, then, was a part of desperation, a last-ditch gamble that had not worked out.

And, Enoch thought, it was ironic that the key of failure lay in the fact that the creature, in its fleeing, had carried the Talisman into the backyard of a sensitive, and on a planet, too, where no one would have thought to look for a sensitive. For, thinking back on it, there could be little doubt that Lucy had sensed the Talisman and had been drawn to it as truly as a magnet would attract a piece of steel. She had known nothing else, perhaps, than that the Talisman had been there and was something she must have, that it was something she had waited for in all her loneliness, without knowing what it was or without hope of finding it. Like a child who sees, quite suddenly, a shiny, glorious bauble on a Christmas tree and knows that it's the grandest thing on Earth and that it must be hers.

This creature lying here, thought Enoch, must have been able and resourceful. For it would have taken great ability and resourcefulness to have stolen the Talisman to start with, to keep it hidden for years, to have penetrated into the secrets and the files of Galactic Central. Would it have been possible, he wondered, if the Talisman had been in effective operation? With an energetic Talisman would the moral laxity and the driving greed been possible to motivate the deed?

But that was ended now. The Talisman had been restored and a new custodian had been found—a deaf-mute girl of Earth,

the humblest of humans. And there would be peace on Earth
and in time the Earth would join the cofraternity of the galaxy.

There were no problems now, he thought. No decisions to be
made. Lucy had taken the decisions from the hands of everyone.

The station would remain and he could unpack the boxes he
had packed and put the journals back on the shelves again. He
could go back to the station once again and settle down and
carry on his work.

I am sorry, he told the huddled shape that lay among the
boulders. *I am sorry that mine was the hand that had to do it
to you.*

He turned away and walked out to where the cliff dropped
straight down to the river flowing at its foot. He raised the rifle
and held it for a moment motionless and then he threw it out
and watched it fall, spinning end for end, the moonlight
glinting off the barrel, saw the tiny splash it made as it struck
the water. And far below, he heard the smug, contented gurgling
of the water as it flowed past this cliff and went on, to the further
ends of Earth.

There would be peace on Earth, he thought; there would be
no war. With Lucy at the conference table, there could be no
thought of war. Even if some ran howling from the fear inside
themselves, a fear and guilt so great that it overrode the glory
and the comfort of the Talisman, there still could be no war.

But it was a long trail yet, a long and lonesome way, before
the brightness of real peace would live in the hearts of man.

Until no man ran howling, wild with fear (any kind of
fear), would there be actual peace. Until the last man threw
away his weapon (any sort of weapon), the tribe of Man could
not be at peace. And a rifle, Enoch told himself, was the least
of the weapons of the Earth, the least of man's inhumanity to
man, no more than a symbol of all the other and more deadly
weapons.

He stood on the rim of the cliff and looked out across the
river and the dark shadow of the wooded valley. His hands felt

strangely empty with the rifle gone, but it seemed that some-where, back there just a way, he had stepped into another field of time, as if an age or day had dropped away and he had come into a place that was shining and brand new and unsullied by any past mistakes.

The river rolled below him and the river did not care. Nothing mattered to the river. It would take the tusk of mastodon, the skull of sabertooth, the rib cage of a man, the dead and sunken tree, the thrown rock or rifle and would swallow each of them and cover them in mud or sand and roll gurgling over them, hiding them from sight.

A million years ago there had been no river here and in a million years to come there might be no river—but in a mil-lion years from now there would be, if not Man, at least a caring thing. And that was the secret of the universe, Enoch told him-self—a thing that went on caring.

He turned slowly from the cliff edge and clambered through the boulders, to go walking up the hill. He heard the tiny scurry-ing of small life rustling through the fallen leaves and once there was the sleepy peeping of an awakened bird and through the entire woods lay the peace and comfort of that glowing light—not so intense, not so deep and bright and so wonderful as when it actually had been there, but a breath of it still left.

He came to the edge of the woods and climbed the field and ahead of him the station stood foursquare upon its ridgetop. And it seemed that it was no longer a station only, but his home as well. Many years ago it had been a home and nothing more and then it had become a way station to the galaxy. But now, although way station still, it was home again.

36

He came into the station and the place was quiet and just a little ghostly in the quietness of it. A lamp burned on his desk and over on the coffee table the little pyramid of spheres was flashing, throwing its many-colored lights, like the crystal balls they'd used in the Roaring Twenties to turn a dance hall into a place of magic. The tiny flickering colors went flitting all about the room, like the dance of a zany band of Technicolor fireflies.

He stood for a moment, indecisive, not knowing what to do. There was something missing and all at once he realized what it was. During all the years there'd been a rifle to hang upon its pegs or to lay across the desk. And now there was no rifle.

He'd have to settle down, he told himself, and get back to work. He'd have to unpack and put the stuff away. He'd have to get the journals written and catch up with his reading. There was a lot to do.

Ulysses and Lucy had left an hour or two before, bound for Galactic Central, but the *feeling* of the Talisman still seemed to linger in the room. Although, perhaps, he thought, not in the room at all, but inside himself. Perhaps it was a feeling that he'd carry with him no matter where he went.

He walked slowly across the room and sat down on the sofa. In front of him the pyramid of spheres was splashing out its crystal shower of colors. He reached out a hand to pick it up, then drew it slowly back. What was the use, he asked himself, of examining it again? If he had not learned its secret the many times before, why should he expect to now?

A pretty thing, he thought, but useless.

He wondered how Lucy might be getting on and knew she

was all right. She'd get along, he told himself, anywhere she went.

Instead of sitting here, he should be getting back to work. There was a lot of catching up to do. And his time would not be his own from now on, for the Earth would be pounding at the door. There would be conferences and meetings and a lot of other things and in a few hours more the newspapers might be here. But before it happened, Ulysses would be back to help him, and perhaps there would be others, too.

In just a little while he'd rustle up some food and then he'd get to work. If he worked far into the night, he could get a good deal done.

Lonely nights, he told himself, were good for work. And it was lonely now, when it should not be lonely. For he no longer was alone, as he had thought he was alone just a few short hours before. Now he had the Earth and the galaxy, Lucy and Ulysses, Winslowe and Lewis and the old philosopher out in the apple orchard.

He rose and walked to the desk and picked up the statuette Winslowe had carved of him. He held it beneath the desk lamp and turned it slowly in his hands. There was, he saw now, a loneliness in that figure, too—the essential loneliness of a man who walked alone.

But he'd had to walk alone. There'd been no other way. There had been no choice. It had been a one-man job. And now the job was—no, not done, for there still was much that must be done. But the first phase of it now was over and the second phase was starting.

He set the statuette back on the desk and remembered that he had not given Winslowe the piece of wood the Thuban traveler had brought. Now he could tell Winslowe where all the wood had come from. They could go through the journals and find the dates and the origin of every stick of it. That would please old Winslowe.

He heard the silken rustle and swung swiftly round.

"Mary!" he cried.

She stood just at the edge of shadow and the flitting colors from the flashing pyramid made her seem like someone who had stepped from fairyland. And that was right, he was thinking wildly, for his lost fairyland was back.

"I had to come," she said. "You were lonely, Enoch, and I could not stay away."

She could not stay away—and that might be true, he thought. For within the conditioning he'd set up there might have been the inescapable compulsion to come whenever she was needed.

It was a trap, he thought, from which neither could escape. There was no free will here, but instead the deadly precision of this blind mechanism he had shaped himself.

She should not come to see him and perhaps she knew this as well as he, but could not help herself. Would this be, he wondered, the way that it would be, forever and forever?

He stood there, frozen, torn by the need of her and the emptiness of her unreality, and she was moving toward him.

She was close to him and in a moment she would stop, for she knew the rules as well as he; she, no more than he, could admit illusion.

But she did not stop. She came so close that he could smell the apple-blossom fragrance of her. She put out a hand and laid it on his arm.

It was no shadow touch and it was no shadow hand. He could feel the pressure of her fingers and the coolness of them.

He stood rigid, with her hand upon his arm.

The flashing light! he thought. The pyramid of spheres!

For now he remembered who had given it to him—one of those aberrant races of the Alphard system. And it had been from the literature of that system that he had learned the art of fairyland. They had tried to help him by giving him the pyramid and he had not understood. There had been a failure of communication —but that was an easy thing to happen. In the Babel of the galaxy, it was easy to misunderstand or simply not to know.

For the pyramid of spheres was a wonderful, and yet a simple, mechanism. It was the fixation agent that banished all illusion, that made a fairyland for real. You made something as you wanted it and then turned on the pyramid and you had what you had made, as real as if it had never been illusion.

Except, he thought, in some things you couldn't fool yourself. You knew it was illusion, even if it should turn real.

He reached out toward her tentatively, but her hand dropped from his arm and she took a slow step backward.

In the silence of the room—the terrible, lonely silence—they stood facing one another while the colored lights ran like playing mice as the pyramid of spheres twirled its everlasting rainbow.

"I am sorry," Mary said, "but it isn't any good. We can't fool ourselves."

He stood mute and shamed.

"I waited for it," she said. "I thought and dreamed about it."

"So did I," said Enoch. "I never thought that it would happen."

And that was it, of course. So long as it could not happen, it was a thing to dream about. It was romantic and far-off and impossible. Perhaps it had been romantic only because it had been so far-off and so impossible.

"As if a doll had come to life," she said, "or a beloved Teddy bear. I am sorry, Enoch, but you could not love a doll or a Teddy bear that had come to life. You always would remember them the way they were before. The doll with the silly, painted smile; the Teddy bear with the stuffing coming out of it."

"No!" cried Enoch. "No!"

"Poor Enoch," she said. "It will be so bad for you. I wish that I could help. You'll have so long to live with it."

"But you!" he cried. "But you? What can you do now?"

It had been she, he thought, who had the courage. The courage that it took to face things as they were.

How, he wondered, had she sensed it? How could she have known?

"I shall go away," she said. "I shall not come back. Even when you need me, I shall not come back. There is no other way."

"But you can't go away," he said. "You are trapped the same as I."

"Isn't it strange," she said, "how it happened to us. Both of us victims of illusion . . ."

"But you," he said. "Not you."

She nodded gravely. "I, the same as you. You can't love the doll you made or I the toymaker. But each of us thought we did; each of us still think we should and are guilty and miserable when we find we can't."

"We could try," said Enoch. "If you would only stay."

"And end up by hating you? And, worse than that, by your hating me. Let us keep the guilt and misery. It is better than the hate."

She moved swiftly and the pyramid of spheres was in her hand and lifted.

"No, not that!" he shouted. "No, Mary . . ."

The pyramid flashed, spinning in the air, and crashed against the fireplace. The flashing lights went out. Something—glass? metal? stone?—tinkled on the floor.

"Mary!" Enoch cried, striding forward in the dark.

But there was no one there.

"Mary!" he shouted, and the shouting was a whimper.

She was gone and she would not be back.

Even when he needed her, she would not be back.

He stood quietly in the dark and silence, and the voice of a century of living seemed to speak to him in a silent language.

All things are hard, it said. There is nothing easy.

There had been the farm girl living down the road, and the southern beauty who had watched him pass her gate, and now there was Mary, gone forever from him.

He turned heavily in the room and moved forward, groping for the table. He found it and switched on the light.

He stood beside the table and looked about the room. In this corner where he stood there once had been a kitchen, and there,

where the fireplace stood, the living room, and it all had changed
—it had been changed for a long time now. But he still could
see it as if it were only yesterday.

All the days were gone and all the people in them.

Only he was left.

He had lost his world. He had left his world behind him.

And, likewise, on this day, had all the others—all the humans
that were alive this moment.

They might not know it yet, but they, too, had left their world
behind them. It would never be the same again.

You said good bye to so many things, to so many loves, to so
many dreams.

"Good bye, Mary," he said. "Forgive me and God keep you."

He sat down at the table and pulled the journal that lay upon
its top in front of him. He flipped it open, searching for the
pages he must fill.

He had work to do.

Now he was ready for it.

He had said his last good bye.